The
Year *of the* Raccoon

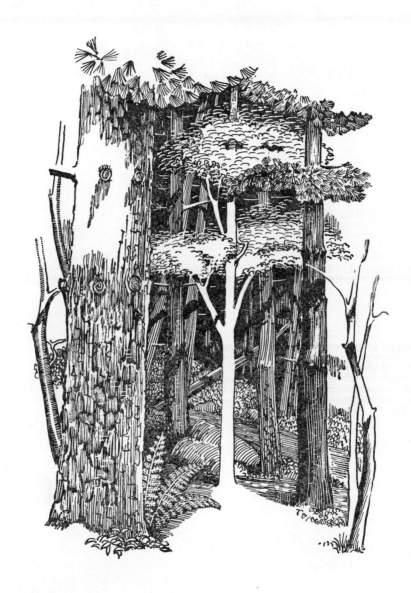

The
Year *of the* Raccoon

LEE KINGMAN

HOUGHTON MIFFLIN COMPANY BOSTON

To
the real
Barney Natti
wherever he is—
and all his
friends

The
Year of the Raccoon

1

JOEY LARKIN's difficult year began on a summer day when he was burning rubbish in the incinerator.

Stuck to the bottom of a wastebasket was one of the cards his parents sent out last Christmas. As he wrenched it up from a splinter in the wicker, the picture on the front tore. His older brother Jerry's face split so unexpectedly it made Joey shudder.

The next face on the Christmas card was his. He thought it was a stupid picture of himself — all ears and limp blond hair over his eyes. He had protested when his mother chose that one to be printed.

"But it's the best one of all three of you," she had explained. "Do you know how many rolls of film it took to produce one picture with all of you in focus and looking human? Three rolls."

"Why don't you send some other kind of card? We're not cute little kids any more."

"Tradition," said his mother. "When you're all through college and have your own families, then I'll stop."

"Ugh," said Joey, feeling helpless. But he hadn't sent any to his friends, even though she ordered extra ones for the boys to use.

He stood now looking at the partly ripped card. The bottom bore a printed message: "Best wishes for a Gay Christmas and a Bright New Year from the Larkins — Rory and Ruth, Jeremy, Joel, and Jock."

Rory! He loved his father's name. It was the kind of name that rolled around on his tongue and came out sounding full of excitement. Why couldn't he have been named for his father! But his mother often said, "One Rory is enough."

He pieced his older brother's face back together and studied it. Jeremy Reed Larkin, II, was named for his grandfather. Jerry was so terrific. He was good-looking — smooth, girls said. He'd been a great Little League baseball player. Maybe he could have gone on to be a pro if he'd stuck with it. But Jerry decided to stick with the piano instead. He couldn't do both. He played so much everyone realized how serious he was about it. It was frightening to have someone in the family serious at eighteen about a career. And good at it. Jerry had played a walloping hard sonata at his High School graduation, and he was going to the Conservatory in New York in the fall.

And Jock was lucky. His name really was Jock, and Jock liked his name. He wasn't much to look at right now. He was too bony for his nine years. His light brown hair was scraggly and he wore glasses which magnified his already large brown eyes. He was a serious little kid. He was scientific. He knew everything about everything — from worms to rockets. He'd begun reading when he was four, so it wasn't just made-up gibberish. He really knew. Very often Jock was just one large continual nonstop un-shut-up-able pain in the neck.

Joel sighed. He hated his name because it tore him in half. Half of him was Joel, as his mother said it, even though he begged her to call him Joey, or Joe.

"If you want me to call you Renfrew of the Mounted Police or Hairbreadth Harry or Ivan Skivitsky-Skavar for a change, I will," she said. "But Joel is such a nice name — and that's who *you* are to me."

But he was Joe and Joey to his friends.

He started to fling the torn card on the fire and saw his mother had written a note on the other side. But

3

there was a large splotch of what looked like coffee spilled over it, which must have been why she'd thrown it away. "Dear Binky," it began. That must be a college friend. She was always mentioning a Binky or a Bendy. There was even someone called Bitty-Betty. So why did she object to a much more honest name like Joey? It was just one more of the things he didn't understand about mothers and his mother in particular.

Joey knew he shouldn't read other people's mail. Jerry beat that into him about the time girls began stuffing notes in his brother's pockets. Notes! They wrote him books! Joey wondered what it would be like to have girls flinging themselves at him all the time the way Jerry did.

But this note in his mother's flighty handwriting wasn't really someone else's mail because it had never been mailed.

The wind shifted and smoke clouded around him, choking him. He stirred the mess in the incinerator with a stick until the flames leaped again.

"Dear Binky," he read slowly. "We hope this year has been as interesting for all the Martins as it has been for the Larkins. Rory still traveling, two thirds of the time. I swore off three committees and ended up on two new ones. Jerry's music thrills us all. He is such a joy — good student, good fun, good disposition, and

4

with talent to match his ambition. Jock, my little one, grows fast and is a very funny boy."

Joey paused. What was funny about insistent old Jock? He could agree with his mother's words about Jerry. Jerry was special. He was even understanding and kind to younger brothers. But Jock seldom seemed funny to him.

He read on. "Jock has great abilities at math and science, and is in an accelerated group at school. I expect to be in awe of him later. Our Joel, who will be fifteen in May, marches on as usual, and we keep hoping a spark will strike someday to get him really interested in his education. His only interests so far are swimming and skiing. If you can think of any good careers built on same, let us know. I suppose with two exceptional boys in the family and their special problems we should be thankful for one nice normal average boy! Can you believe next June will bring our 20th reunion? See you there. Love, Ruth."

Joey read the words again. So he was a nice normal average boy. Why then did each word feel like a knife wound?

He didn't know, unless it was because everyone in the family was special in some way, except for him. But his mother made it sound as if just because he wasn't brilliant, he didn't really belong to them at all. She might just as well have written "and then of course

5

we have dull old Joel, too, but we haven't the vaguest idea of what to do with him and he doesn't seem to have any idea of what to do with himself. So there he is — that's all, and we're stuck with him."

Suddenly he tore the rest of the card into pieces again and again and flung them on the fire. A draft caught them and they swirled up like rebellious snowflakes that wouldn't fall down. He struck at them with the stick.

"Joel!" His mother's sudden unexpected call made him jump. Why did she have to tell all those family matters on Christmas cards anyway? Up until now he'd managed all right. He liked to play football and basketball and eat and horse around with his friends. He had a good enough time and he got by in school. What was so terrible about being called a nice normal average boy? It was certainly a lot better than someone thinking he was real far out or maybe queer. She ought to be thankful he was an average boy. She shouldn't make it sound as if he were flunking life already!

"Joel?"

"Here!" he yelled. "Burning the trash."

"I'm sending Jock out with more. When you finish, you can have free time till supper."

Jock came slowly around the corner. He was reading a pamphlet propped in the top of the plastic wastebasket he clutched to his stomach. He didn't even bother to look where he was going, so he tripped over the hose.

"Watch it!" Joey said flatly. "Or you're going to step on every one of those new lettuce plants."

"Tell me how many degrees to turn, then," Jock said, and went right on reading.

Joey sighed. Was that the kind of thing his mother called funny? Or did it just make Jock more special? Different. Not odd, of course. Just lovable and special and funny — to her.

"Oh, forty-five degrees." That should take Jock across the carrots without too much havoc. He turned to stir the incinerator again and Jock butted him with the wastebasket.

"Oops! Sorry," said Jock, rescuing the pamphlet before Joey threw it on the flames.

"Do you have to read even when you're going somewhere?"

"That's an interesting article. On the Merchant Marine. You threw it away after you did your career booklet for school. Can I keep it?"

"You'll never have time to read half the stuff falling off your shelves now."

"Yes, I will. Didn't you see me practicing reading while I walked?"

"Sure. If I hadn't been in the way, you would have fallen into the incinerator."

"I'm developing my radar sensitivity. With practice

I should be able intuitively to stop before bumping, even while I concentrate on something else. You know what I heard about the man who invented Cybernetics?"

Joey didn't answer because Jock's questions, when he was well launched on a subject, were purely rhetorical.

"He was a professor at a big university and he read all the time. When he changed classes, he ran a pencil along the wall and when the pencil went around a corner, he followed it. And he ended up in his next classroom all right, and probably read fifty or sixty pages while he was getting there."

"He could have ended up turning pages in a broom closet, you know."

"Well, he didn't!" said Jock indignantly. "And I'll bet I can do it better than he could in a very little while."

"You probably can." Joel emptied the plastic wastebasket and slammed it upside down over Jock's head. Most brothers would call that an invitation to a fight, mock or real — a good excuse to dance around and wrestle, trade some pent-up remarks and throw in a few longed-for socks. But not Jock. It was just one of the things that frustrated Joey.

"Hey! This ought to be a good radar test," Jock squeaked from under the basket. "Steer me toward the house and I'll see if plastic dims my sensitivity."

8

But Joel had spent an hour weeding that morning and he didn't want his neat work trampled by Jock's experimenting feet until his father had inspected the garden. At least they all hoped his father would return from Mexico that night.

He grabbed the basket and threw it as far as he could toward the lawn. It fell with a disappointing plop into the parsley border.

"Too bad," said Jock. "You throw much better than that as a rule. But there's all kinds of resistance to a hollow object. You really ought to stop and figure out what you're up against before you throw it. Want to play catch?"

"Not with you."

"Why not?"

"Because you'd be more interested in some old mathematical curve the ball was making than in helping me improve my pitching. No thanks. I'm going for a walk in the woods."

"I'll come with you," Jock offered. He skipped the way he did when he was eager to do something. "I'll look for salamanders."

"You go one way and I'll go the other, then."

"Don't you want me to come with you?" Jock blinked in surprise. "I can tell you where to look. With two of us we can find twice as many."

Jock's insistence was almost more than Joel could bear. "You can be awfully dumb for someone who's so brilliant! Can't you see I want to be by myself? I don't want any scientific chatter-machine running along beside me, telling me what to do. I'm just a normal average dumb boy and I want to take a walk in the woods all by my average self — all right?"

"Sure," said Jock, retreating a little. "But I don't see what you're mad about. I didn't say you were stupid or anything."

"Well, take the wastebaskets in to Mum and tell her I'll be back to supper. I think."

For once Jock did as he was told without discussing it. But he turned back and looked at Joel, a puzzled frown distorting his small face.

Joey slipped through the barred gate and wandered up the dirt road to the woods. On his right curved the pond, built by bulldozing a good-sized waterhole and diverting a brook. Joey remembered that project of two years ago with delight. The bulldozer was a tremendous one, and he'd been allowed to sit with the driver and pull all sorts of levers. And Joey had even figured out a better course for the brook than his father had planned.

Once the pond was filled, the whole family claimed it — for wake-up plunges in the morning and cooling-off dips at night, and for skating in winter. His father put wood-duck boxes by it and Jock stocked it with the turtles he found, carefully marking each one with his initials and the date, and listing them in a notebook. Jock kept lists of everything.

Beyond the pond stretched the woods. "Wild woods when we came fifteen years ago," his father liked to point out to visitors. "But we've tamed them. I've got over a hundred acres now in trees." There was an official sign by their front gate that read AMERICAN TREE FARM ASSOCIATION.

The farm was his father's hobby. "I do so much traveling for my job that I need thousands of roots at home," Mr. Larkin joked.

He was a consultant for a famous company which took on scientific and industrial problems for other companies. Since he traveled all over the world for more than half of each year, it was fortunate he could hire help to do most of the actual work around the place.

Joey could hear a chain saw whining now. Reino, the sturdy Finn who carried out his father's plans, was cleaning dead trees out of a swampy patch. In the morning Reino liked Joey's company and enjoyed talking. But by afternoon, especially hot afternoons, Reino said he was too tired to speak English.

"If you want to trim branches and don't talk to me, fine," he'd say. Yet he always could find some strong English words if Joey didn't trim the branches close enough. Reino conveniently forgot his English when

Jock was around, just so he wouldn't have to answer the questions.

Joey looked at his watch. It was three-thirty, almost Reino's quitting time, and with this heat he probably wouldn't even grunt a greeting. So Joey turned off the path and climbed to the top of a large boulder, surrounded so closely by cedar trees that it was like being inside a green tower. For a while he felt cool.

Jerry had used this rock as a hideaway before him. Joey wondered if he talked to his brother, if Jerry would understand how Joey felt about being the family disappointment. But how could you ask a young man so full of enthusiasm for music that he practiced seven hours a day, if he thought just dreaming around for fourteen hours a day was wrong? Joey figured out he spent eight hours sleeping and two hours eating out of each twenty-four. That left fourteen — and what did he really do with them?

Something else his mother wrote on the card returned to bother him. "We keep hoping a spark will strike someday to get him really interested in his education." Didn't she think it bothered him — now and then — worrying about what he was going to do? Three more years and he'd be through High School. There were times when he felt panicky just thinking about it.

He threw back his head and stared up the tunnel of green to the bright sky. "Well, here I am," he said out loud. "Waiting for a spark to strike. How about that!"

There wasn't a sound in the drowsy woods. The whine of the saw stopped. Birds and squirrels found it too hot to scurry. No matter how much Joey wished it, no magic sign or omen would suddenly appear to help him solve his present and his future. No Excalibur would give him authority to be a champion.

Lichens on the rock scratched his hands. It was all too quiet and made him restless. He decided to carry the chain saw back for Reino and ask him to look at the work he'd done in the garden. Then in case Dad didn't return, someone would appreciate and report on his work.

Sliding off the rock, he cut through a path and found Reino checking up on his tools.

"Too hot for that saw today. She quit. Hope your father has time to catch up on all the tinkering waiting for him."

"Want me to carry it?"

"Make you stronger, huh? Boys your age always heaving and lifting. You get as good muscles chopping wood." Reino grinned. He was in his sixties and barrel-shaped, but still muscle-conscious. He enjoyed teasing Joey about the set of weights he kept in the garage and worked out with when he was in the mood.

"I'm going to dig out some swamp cranberry. Take it back and see if it will grow by my brook."

The swamp was dry this time of year, which made it easy to haul out the dead maples and brush. Reino dug into a clump of stiff grasses to find the roots of a scraggly cranberry.

But the shoveling was tough. Finally he stood on the spade and wiggled it back and forth to break out the clump.

"Hey!" Reino dropped the shovel and knelt down, pulling apart the tangle of grass. "Look what we got here!" He scooped up five naked baby things and held them out. Joey stared at them.

Against Reino's rough thick hands, their skin was as fragile as a pink balloon. He could see each shivering breath being pulled out of their trembling chests. There was a slight brownish fuzz over their backs and heads. They wiggled and pushed against each other.

Joey carefully unwrapped one from its brothers. It was incredible that such a limp scrap could be alive. With its eyes shut, it seemed as if the little thing had not yet taken on the real world, but was still in a tight world of its own. A tiny claw flicked helplessly up and down.

"No long tail, so they're not mice. What are they?" Joey asked.

"See the ears? Baby rabbits." Reino stooped to put them back in the tangled grass nest he had nearly trampled.

"Do wild rabbits make good pets?"

14

Reino shrugged. "Your father doesn't like them in the garden."

"I wouldn't let them near the garden." Joey ran a finger down the back of the creature in his hand. It was like stroking a bubble — the whole thing might disappear in an instant. "Let me borrow your cap. I want to take two or three home."

Reino's hat was his badge of office as a woodsman. Winter and summer he always wore a visored cap which he took off only when Mrs. Larkin asked him in for coffee. Then he sat with it between his knees.

Reino hesitated. "You think your ma will like you to bring home those blind-naked rabbits?"

"I don't know. But she's always encouraged us to love animals. Look at all the ones we've tried. Mice, hamsters, guinea pigs and tame rabbits. But something always happened to them."

Reino took off his cap. Joey put three gasping babies into it. The other two he tucked back in the nest. Then, hat in one hand, chain saw in the other, he strode off toward the house.

"Once — just once — I'd like to bring up a wild animal and have it my pet. I'd like to do something that Jerry hasn't done and Jock hasn't done either."

At the house, Joey gently transferred the babies to a shoebox lined with crumpled paper towels. Then he took the cap back to Reino, who was inspecting Joey's work in the garden.

15

"Better water those lettuce plants now it's cooler. Want to drive me to the gate?"

Joey hesitated. He could drive the pick-up truck anywhere on the place. Since he was twelve some of his happiest hours were spent bombing, as he called it, the truck around the woods roads, backing, turning and steering through tight spots to his heart's content.

"If it's too hot for you to walk home, Reino, why don't I get Jerry to drive you all the way, instead of just me taking you to the gate? Mum's gone out, and I think I ought to feed those rabbits."

They stood still and listened. Jerry's piano practice was so constant that it often became a background noise to them on hot days when the windows were open. Jerry worked now on some chords, striking them over and over. Joey looked at this watch. "Four-thirty. He's been practicing since lunch. Boy! How he can do it day after day beats me. He doesn't even take time off to go sailing or go to the movies any more. He's nuts."

"Some pretty strong nuts get famous," said Reino. "I'm not in a hurry. I'll walk. See you in the morning, if you're not too busy feeding those rabbits."

Joey grinned and hurried inside. He finally found an eyedropper in the medicine cabinet and rinsed it out.

In the kitchen Jock was constructing a triple-decker sandwich. He watched Joey pour milk into a small saucer. "You better boil that eyedropper," Jock instructed him. "And make up a formula — say, canned milk and Karo syrup and a vitamin pill."

"Why should I be all that fussy for wild animals? Their mother brings them up in some pretty unsterilized places."

"That's the eyedropper Mum used to put stuff in my eyes for pink-eye. You want pink-eyed rabbits with pink-eye? And anybody knows mother's milk, even if it's rabbit milk, has qualities in it cow's milk doesn't have."

"I should think anything that would bring up a cow could bring up a rabbit. Bigger and better."

But Joey boiled the eyedropper, and he ground up a vitamin pill and mixed it with some Karo and canned milk, so if the rabbits died, Jock couldn't say, "I told you so."

He picked up one of the babies and it wasn't even as long as the palm of his hand. But whenever he tried to put the eyedropper in its mouth, it pushed up its scrappy paws in protest and pulled its head back out of the way.

"What a nutty thing," said Joey. "Here I am trying to feed it and it's trying to get away." Then he remembered how he'd kept his baby mouse from struggling when he'd fed it. "Jock — get me some Kleenex, please."

When Jock brought the Kleenex, Joey wrapped the little animal up, all but his head. Then he could con-

17

centrate on gently pushing its small jaws apart with the dropper and squeezing in a bit of milk.

"Hey — you can watch the milk going down inside his neck, his skin is so thin."

Joey put the rabbit back in the box and started to unwrap it from the Kleenex, which clung where milk had dribbled down it.

"He looks like a mummy," said Jock. "Remember the Mummied Mouse?"

"Yeah." Joey still felt badly about that. Three years ago Reino had brought in a handful of deer-mouse babies. They were even tinier than the rabbits, but not as limp and frail. Joey had kept one to try and raise a pet. He fed it faithfully for four days, and then someone interrupted him and he left it wrapped up in the wet Kleenex. When he remembered, it was blue and colder than an ice cube. He warmed it in his hands and then in a nest of cotton over a light bulb. But it died. "Pneumonia," Jock had diagnosed. In his heart Joey suffered because it was his neglect. They put it in Animal Rest — a plot behind the garage where they buried dead birds found around the yard and the tame rabbits that had keeled over sideways from some disease and Jerry's hamster that had died of old age. And Gidney — the guinea pig murdered by a dog.

That had been such a horrid day that Joey still remembered it vividly. It was the boys' first brush with violent death of a being they loved. They had been so upset that Mrs. Larkin decreed a formal funeral service just to give them something to do. Their cousin Tim, who was on vacation from military school, stood at attention in his uniform, and their father in a frock coat and tall beaver hat from the costume box read a poem about "Little things that run and quail." Their mother even put on a hat for the occasion. Jerry had attempted Taps on a bugle. It had been a fitting and solemn time, until the evening mosquitoes suddenly descended and sent them slapping madly from the scene. The special stone, flecked with shiny mica, was still in place. Joey was determined that these wild rabbits were not going to end up in Animal Rest.

"If Dad comes home, I'll borrow his travel alarm clock and wake myself up at midnight and at four to feed them," he told Jock.

"Well, don't wake me up."

"Why not? You wake me up early every morning, just because you want to talk."

It irked Joey more and more to share a room with Jock. The play area gaily defined in the floor tile, where they once used trucks and building sets, now seemed insultingly young. In Jock's corner stood a large tropical aquarium, which Joey didn't mind too much. The fish were soothing company and the device that kept air circulating through the water made a nightly lullaby. "Glub-glub," sang the tank. "Bur-gubble, ger-plup. Glub, glup."

Beside the aquarium was a tank full of damp dirt and moss, twigs and rocks, where Jock housed salamanders and visiting turtles. Then there were two chests of all kinds of things, because Jock had only to mention something and wonder how it worked and Mrs. Larkin would buy it for him.

He had an abacus, a slide rule and a microscope with all kinds of slides. He had a spectroscopic lab kit and a Morse code sender and collections of rocks and butterflies. He puttered around like an old man in a laboratory.

As Joey tried to reach his bedside table and leave the rabbits and their night's supply of formula there, he kicked at a pile of Jock's old *National Geographics.* They avalanched over the floor.

"Have you got slippery magazines!"

"Don't complain," Jock warned. "Or I'll tell Mum about the five hundred and ten comics you have under your bed."

Joey grunted. All kinds of things stuck out from under his bed, where he kicked them for safe keeping. In season there were hockey sticks, pucks, footballs, basketballs, baseball bats and gloves, flippers and snorkels. There was even a boomerang his father had brought from Australia.

Della, who came two days a week to clean, made a pact with the boys. Anything they wanted to save had to be on a shelf, in a box or under a bed on Tuesdays and Fridays, or she could throw it away.

Jerry stuck his head in the door. "Didn't you guys see the instructions posted in the hall?"

"No. Mum said free time till supper."

"That's out. Dad called. She's driving to pick him up at the airport. Back about seven-thirty. We've got chores and we'd better start now."

Joey tucked the rabbit box under one arm, so if they started squeaking he'd know. They read off the orders. "Joel — case garden for salad stuff. Pick. Wash. Dry. Jock, set table in dining room. Celebratious-like. Jerry, drive to Bartlett's before closing and pick up steaks. All ordered."

Jerry looked at the clock. "I can just make it." He turned quickly and nearly knocked the box from Joey's arm. "Sorry — are you playing shoe store?"

Jocy pulled back the paper and showed him the bony heads and scrawny bodies.

"Yuk!" said Jerry, wrinkling his nose in distaste. "Only their mother could love them."

"Then don't breathe all over them if you don't like them. I'm mother."

"Are they wild and woodsy?"

"Rabbits."

21

"Will you never learn!" Jerry shook his head. "But maybe you'll grow up to be the Dr. Spock of the Animal Kingdom."

"Joel's infant mortality rate is too high," Jock decided. "He's lost too many cases."

"Rub it in some more!" Joey glowered at Jock. "You may be smart, but boy! your glasses are dirty."

"I'm glad Daddy's almost home," said Jock soberly. "You've been picking on me all week."

"Oh? You can feel it through your super-sensitive radar system?"

"Thaw it out!" Jerry grabbed the key to the station wagon from the rack below the bulletin board. "We have half an hour to roll out the red carpet. Dad's been gone six whole weeks this time. He may come home with white hair and a beard. Scramble!"

Joey put the box down between the lettuce rows and enviously watched Jerry drive away. He could hardly wait to be sixteen and earn his driver's license. Then maybe he'd have something beside agricultural chores. He had complained before his father left on this last trip about being stuck in the garden, while Jerry chauffeured and Jock invented.

"You're the only one who knows lettuce from endive," his father praised him. "You make sense out of the whole weedy outburst. Jerry starts picking with some concerto in his head and next thing you know he's acting like a metronome and pulling up any old

22

thing just so he doesn't miss a beat. And old Jock is sitting there twenty minutes without moving — watching a leaf grow. No, without you, Joe, we'd starve."

Joey glowed, for his father seldom lavished praise on him. But the praise wore thin during six monotonous weeks of weeding.

When he asked his mother if he couldn't swap off just for a week, she told him no one could produce such beautiful vegetables as he did. Just for fun she picked a superb head of curly bronze lettuce, tied a gorgeous brown satin bow around the stalk and carried it as a bouquet to a dinner party. "They all loved it, Joel!" she reported.

"The lettuce? Or just because you did something none of them had thought of?"

"Joel! You work hard in that garden. Why can't you take pride in it? Growing a lovely head of lettuce is just as wonderful as Jerry's playing a piece on the piano. Or Jock's building a robot control station."

"Is it? Or are you just trying to cheer me up by making a big thing out of it?"

"What's happened to my only even-tempered happy-go-lucky member of the family!" Mrs. Larkin exclaimed. "Right now you seem out of tune. Please don't go sitting in your shell with the door all shut."

"Shells don't have doors, Mum."

"No, in your mind they couldn't. You know, each one of you boys thinks so differently. It's fascinating."

She stopped what she was doing long enough to stare at him. "But I never expected you to turn moody."

"If you moved me out of Jock's room — and out of the garden — I'd get unmoody."

"Nobody ever solved anything by running away from it."

"Mum, I don't want to solve Jock. I just want to get away from him once in a while. Like twenty-three hours out of twenty-four."

"You're serious?"

"Never more."

"All right. We'll talk to Dad about it when he comes home."

Joey wondered if Dad would come home in such a burst of enthusiasm if he knew all the things that awaited him to be fixed, from chain saws to emotions. But it was always the same way. No matter what exotic-sounding spot he'd been in, he'd arrive shouting that there was absolutely no place like home and he was a fool, an unmitigated fool, to go away at all. He'd quit his job tomorrow and never leave again!

There was the brassy root-a-toot-toot of the horn on the Porsche. Dad was early! He was back!

Joey dropped the salad stuff in a heap and ran around the house. His father was big and handsome and so tan that his face was a startling contrast to his light tropical suit and the gleaming white Porsche from which he sprang. It struck Joey — who had gone along unenthusiastically when his mother took the boys to the opera — that his father looked like the Knight Lohengrin arising from the white swan.

"Hail the Family Hero!" yelled Joey and flung himself at Mr. Larkin's torso.

"Joe!" His father squeezed him just about breathless. "You have expanded again. Turn around. All in proportion, too. Great job, Joey. Mum tells me you've been the level-headed help while I was gone. And the garden is terrific, she says — thanks to you."

Joey grinned. Dad made it all sound worthwhile, the whole six grubby weeks.

Jerry arrived, tooting the station wagon horn in salute. Jock came skittering out. Mr. Larkin picked him up as if he were still a little kid. "How's the genius? What have you invented this time?" he kidded.

But the trouble with Jock was he took everything seriously and as usual he had invented something. He explained it earnestly while Dad lugged him into the house. Jerry rushed the steaks in. Joey reached into the Porsche and pulled out Dad's enormous traveling bag.

"Oh, isn't it good to have Dad home!" said Mrs. Larkin.

"Mum, did you ask him if I could move out of Jock's room?"

"Honey, he's only just off the plane. We can let our problems wait till tomorrow."

"If he stays around that long."

"Joel! What is the matter with you today? I know Dad's not being here very often when we need him is hard on you boys. But you are the one who is out of step right now. Out of step with the whole family. Joel — look at me."

Joey didn't want to look at her. But it was something she had made the boys do from the time they were tiny. She made them look her right in the eye when she was trying to find out something. She was slender and she looked small when she stood next to Dad. She was blonde and if she didn't go around talking about it, no one would dream she'd been out of college twenty years. She loved paintings and books, music, theater, ballet and clothes. But she could be as relentless as a drill sergeant.

The habit she'd instilled was too strong. He couldn't help meeting her gaze. But she was smiling, not frowning at him.

"I'm sorry if you have a lot of bothers. I promise just as soon as Dad's ready for family matters, we'll talk. You and Dad should go off by yourselves, too. Oh, my — Joel! We're not even eye-level any more. I have to look up to you, and you're looking down at me." She just stood there and sighed, as if it were a tragic discovery.

Joey never liked being stared at. "I'll go get the salad stuff. I forgot it in the garden, and I forgot the rabbits."

"What rabbits?" asked his mother uneasily.

But Mr. Larkin was calling and Joey escaped. He took the box back to the bedroom and then dumped the salad stuff in the sink. They were all busy in the kitchen except Jock, who wouldn't let anyone in the dining room. "It's a party and I'm fixing up the table," he announced.

Mr. Larkin and Jerry watched the steaks. At last everything was ready.

"Come on, Jock. Open up."

"Wait till I light the candles."

When he opened the door, Jerry said, "Wow!"

Mrs. Larkin said, "How ingenious!"

Joey groaned, and Mr. Larkin said, "I feel like the Maharajah of Kandaipur or such."

The candles were indeed lit, revolving about the table in the flat cars of Joey's old electric train, while salts and peppers rode by on top of baggage cars. It was very effective, but the grinding buzz of the cars on the track grew more and more like the wince of chalk on a blackboard.

After a while Jerry said, "Could we please have a railroad strike? I'm getting dizzy."

Reluctantly Jock unplugged his centerpiece. Then Dad told them all about the job in a remote moun-

27

tain section of Mexico. He distributed his presents. "Here's a piece of pre-Columbian pottery for Mum," he said, carefully handing out a jolly little terra cotta fellow. "And Jock, here are some butterfly specimens. Ones you don't see around here. Jerry, here's a flute the Indians use. You need a recess from that piano. Joe, here's a pair of *huaraches* — leather sandals the Mexicans wear. And now I suddenly have a thumping suspicion that they're going to be too small."

Joey placed them on the rug and tried to shove his foot all the way into one. It just wouldn't go.

"I'm sorry," said his father. "I have goofed."

"That's all right." Joey tried to hide his disappointment. "You couldn't know I'd grow that much in six weeks."

"Jock's feet are smaller," said Mrs. Larkin, being practical. "Give Joel the butterflies and Jock the *huaraches*."

"But Joey doesn't collect butterflies and I do," said Jock.

"And I'm all feet and you're not," said Joey, standing up. "May I be excused? I've got to feed my rabbits."

"Are we trying livestock again?" asked Mr. Larkin. "What kind this time?"

"Wild ones. Cottontails." Joey picked up his plate.

"Are their eyes open yet?" asked Mrs. Larkin hope-

28

fully. "I mean, are they big enough so they might survive if you put a lot of time into them?" She remembered the Mummied Mouse only too well.

"No. But I've named them," said Joey defiantly. "So I expect to pull them through."

"What'd you name them?" asked Jock.

"Prancer. Donder. And Blitzen. And don't tell me they aren't rabbits' names," he added as Jock opened his mouth. "Because it's one thing — dumb as I am — that I know."

He heard nothing but silence behind him as he marched down the hall. But the triumph of momentarily subduing them was lost when he realized the silence came from their bewilderment. And if they — all the smart ones — didn't know why he felt so miserable, then what hope was there for him to find out for himself?

2

THE DAY Mr. Larkin took Joey out deep-sea fishing on a friend's tuna boat was lazy. His father was so relaxed, Joey didn't know whether to bring up his frustrations or not. Out there in the sparkle of sea and gay sky his problems didn't even seem so heavy. But when they came in sight of land he hunched up and frowned again. Then his father decided it was time to talk.

"Joe, your mother tells me you and Jocko are incompatible." Mr. Larkin, once he considered a problem, plunged right in. "Your temperaments are certainly different, and there's no doubt that with five and a half years between you your interests are different, too. She

30

says you'd like your quarters anywhere but with Jock. So you take the screened porch and use a sleeping bag on the hammock. When Jerry leaves in September, you can take over his room."

Joey wondered how his father always made problems sound so easy to solve. "Dad, what do you do when a problem *really* bugs you and you don't know what to do?"

"I don't start defeating myself by listing all the things I think I can't do. I look for schemes that will work and find out which is best. That's the only way."

"And it always works?"

"Usually. Not always. Take today. I was positive I'd come home with a tremendous tuna. We didn't even catch a dog fish."

On the way home, they stopped for a supper of fried clams. Halfway through Joey felt fortified enough to ask, "Dad, do you worry about me because I don't know what I'm going to do when I finish High School? I mean — if I'm going to college or into the service or what kind of a job I'll get?"

"I'm not worried about your going to college. Of course you'll go."

"I don't know. I thought maybe by now somebody could tell me what I was good at and then tell me what I ought to do. But I'm not very good at anything. Except the garden. And I sure don't want to be stuck with that all my life. So I may not be good enough to get into college. At least the kind of college you think of as college. You know, Harvard, Yale, like that. So then what do I do?"

"Hmmmmm," said Mr. Larkin. His father kept on eating clams but he had what Joey called his computer face on. He seemed to be feeding facts through his mind and listening to them sort out significantly. Then he recognized the need for one more fact.

"*Why* do you think you're no good at anything?"

"Well, I'm just not. I don't have A's in school like Jerry or Jock. Mine are mostly C's and some D's. Jerry knows he's going to be a pianist. Jock could be any kind of scientist or a mathematician. What can I do?"

"First," said his father sternly, "you can quit feeling sorry for yourself because Jerry and Jock are good at some things you're not good at. They might just grow up lop-sided, narrow-minded and too specialized, although I doubt it. Larkins are always vigorous people with lots of interests. Second, you can try all sorts of interesting things, until you find one that fits. Third, keep aiming at college and intend to make it. Every time you miss something or drop a subject, you close another door on some aspect of your life. You want to keep as many doors open as you can. Now there's no reason for you not to buck up and have confidence in yourself. You can do anything you really want to do."

When his father talked that way, Joey was sure he could. Mr. Larkin had an excess of enthusiasm which always swept Joey up, too. But where could he use it? What could he do? All he knew was that he wanted terribly to prove to his father that he could do something and do it well — and that his father expected him to be a success at something. As he implied, Larkins were never failures.

Mrs. Larkin was playing cribbage with Jock on the porch when they wandered home. "Finish up, Mum!" Joey cried. "You're sitting in my room. Dad says for me to take over the porch."

"I'll move out here, too," said Jock. "I like to sleep out."

"No," decided Mr. Larkin. "Whatever Joey does, he's going to do it without you."

"Why?" Jock was hurt.

"Because it's time he is recognized as an individual in this family. Not just as Middle Brother, like the Chinese."

"Great!" Joey threw his swordfisherman's cap onto the hammock. "Mind if I start moving now?"

"Do let us finish our game. I'm the closest I've ever come to double-skunking Jock."

Joey enjoyed moving out of Jock's room so much he forgot all about the rabbits. When his mother and Jerry had offered to look out for them so he could go fishing, he had left the box on the kitchen table with a jar of formula, a clean eyedropper and instructions to feed when hungry. One rabbit had been apathetic when he fed it that morning. He had to force its jaws open and then the milk bubbled out of its nose. But three days of feeding was filling them out, and the grayish-brownish fuzz bloomed over their backs and bellies. Their ears showed the brighter pink of minute veins. He felt those secret heavy eyelids would snap open any minute. He expected that to be momentous, as if once they saw eye to eye there would be an unbreakable bond between them.

He was just flipping his sleeping bag onto the hammock when Jerry stepped onto the porch, the box in his hands.

"Say, Joey — I feel awful, but I forgot about these things. Mum fed them at noontime and then she went off to the beach with Jock. I put the box right on the piano where I'd be sure to see it and remember. But I looked right through it, I guess. So they haven't been fed since noon. I'm really sorry."

"Are they dead?" Joey felt the pain of panic in his stomach as he grabbed the box.

"I don't know. I didn't want to look."

"You just didn't want to feed them because they still look uncooked and you didn't want to hold them," Joey muttered. He pulled back the crumpled paper.

"It wasn't that at all," explained Jerry. "I was working hard and I just plain forgot. That one's all right yet. It's wiggling."

But Joey poked unhappily at the other two. They were cold and stiff. "Thanks a bunch. A great big bunch. Two of them are done for." A sad chill ran through him, looking at the helpless scraps in his hands.

"I'm sorry. Look — I'll get the stuff to feed the wiggly one. It's on the piano."

"Never mind. I'd rather you took this box out to the garage and dug a hole for them in the morning."

"All right."

Joey took the live rabbit, which wasn't very warm, and hurried to the Music Room. He scuffled around among stacks of music to find the milk. After he fed it, he put the lone rabbit in a small box, packed with cotton balls, and covered it all with a woolen scarf. Then he put it on a chair by the hammock and crawled into his sleeping bag.

He missed the burbling of the fish tank. An owl hooted insistently in the woods, and a fox uttered his short sharp bark, first near and then far. There were rustlings and scrapings through the shrubs and flowers near the house, as the whiff of a skunk passed by. Joey felt so sweaty he unzipped his sleeping bag.

At last he fell asleep, only to be awakened as the first birds chattered with the lifting light. A pair of wrens sounded as if they were arguing and neither would give in. Joey tried to fall asleep with his fingers in his ears, but that was too uncomfortable.

He greeted a flaming sunrise with tired blinking eyes. But he greeted it blissfully alone, without Jock. At least he had a half hour of groggy peace until Jock arrived in his pajamas, sipping on a glass of orange juice and announcing he was lonely.

"As long as you're awake, will you play Scrabble with me?"

"At six-thirty in the morning?" Joey yawned. "I've got to feed my rabbit."

"Jerry told me two died. He and I are going to bury them after breakfast. I'll sing a hymn if you like. Which rabbit is left?"

"Blitzen."

"Let's see!"

They unpacked the rabbit from its nest. For the first time it felt babyish and cuddly. "His ears look more rabbity every day," Joey said proudly.

"Too bad you only have one left," Jock said. But despite his promise that it would be a fine ceremony, Joey did not attend the burial.

For two days all went well. Joey found he could keep the rabbit warm in his shirt pocket, so he took it along as he followed his father through the woods. Mr. Larkin was mapping out new tree plantings and roads to cut for fire breaks. Reino tramped along with them, pointing out trees where a red squirrel had

36

nipped off the crucial new growth. Lancelot, the Irish setter, raced back and forth, impatient with them for stopping so often.

Joey was content just being there and listening. He wished for his father's ability to make decisions quickly.

"Why are you staring at me?" Mr. Larkin suddenly asked Joey.

"I didn't know I was," Joey said. But each time his father came home he stored up new things about him in his mind. If only his father's brilliance and ability and effervescent personality would rub off on him! If he could just have some of that confidence, how it would help.

"It's nice to have a son who likes to stalk around the woods with me." Mr. Larkin threw an arm around Joey. "Sometimes I don't think Jock or Jerry have had fresh air in their lungs for days. And they never have time for their old man the way you do, Joe. I wish I could take you along on some of my trips. If I can work out a short trip — say, two weeks some-where — would you come with me?"

Joe was speechless. He just nodded at his father and couldn't tell for a minute whether it was the rab-bit scrabbling about in his pocket or his heartbeat revving up excitedly. As far as he knew, his father had never even suggested that the other boys go any-where with him — ever.

"I'll be off to Iceland soon. I'll see what I can do," Mr. Larkin promised.

"You go to Finland, Mr. Larkin, you can take me," Reino chuckled.

"That I'll do," Mr. Larkin promised just as heartily.

Joey wandered through the rest of the day in a daze of hope and joy. He never talked about his deepest hopes, partly because Jerry and Jock did so much of the family talking he'd long ago given up trying to be heard, unless it were something short and important. Also he didn't want anyone to take his vague idealistic dreams apart by telling him why they might not work, or how he could achieve something else quicker and better. So he never talked about how much he idolized his father. He kept Mr. Larkin's idea of a trip together as a secret joy.

To complete his feeling of happiness the rabbit was at last a thoroughly recognizable rabbit, and while Joey was feeding it that evening, its eyes began to open.

"Hey, look, Jock! His eyelids are unsticking!" Joey shared this triumph because he knew no one in the family had expected any of the rabbits to live that long.

They watched the opened slit widen a bit, as if the rabbit were not sure he really wanted to see the world.

"I thought his eyelids would just snap open with a

boing — like a window shade when it suddenly rolls up," Jock said in disappointment. But the rabbit seemed to be rolling up his eyelids by some slow inside process, so after a while Jock went off. Joe sat and stared at the rabbit until at last they were eye to eye, looking at each other. When he heard his mother and father come in, he called them out to the porch.

"Look at Blitzen!"

The miniature rabbit sat in the palm of his hand. The subtle shadings of brown and gray and white fur gave him roundness and form. His ears were alert. There was the sheerest hint of whiskers at his pink nose. He looked out at them in complete calm from behind the now bright eyes.

"Joel!" Mrs. Larkin was amazed. "He's just precious! You know what he reminds me of? A wood engraving by Dürer that always looked more like a rabbit than any rabbit ought to look. I mean — this one is like a little piece of perfection."

"You want to hold him?"

"All right. He won't jump off my hand?"

"He hasn't yet."

"Wait till I get my camera!" Mr. Larkin rushed off. Even when the flashbulbs sparkled off, the rabbit just crouched there without moving.

"You know, I thought once his eyes opened, I could see inside of him sort of," Joey laughed. "Sort of see

39

why he was, I guess. But when you get those eyes staring back at you, you realize he's just somebody else trying to see into you."

"A profound observation, that!" Mr. Larkin nodded approvingly. "Joe, you may turn out to be a philosopher or a naturalist yet."

Joey laughed uncomfortably. He rarely expressed any of the observations he made about people or events, because he expected to be laughed at rather than lauded. And to have his father take one of his observations and make a big thing out of it scared him. Also, it was sometimes hard to tell when his father was being sincere, and when he was too carried away by enthusiasm.

Now that Joey was used to the night noises of the woods around him, he just set the hammock to swinging very slowly when he went to bed and fell asleep in no time. Somewhere in the night Joey thought he heard the phone ring. But it only half-awakened him for a drowsy moment. The air smelt damp with fog and he burrowed farther into the bag. There was no sunrise to pry his eyes open, so he woke with a heart-stopping shudder as his father shook him.

"Joe, old boy! Just time to say goodby. Got a hurry-up call in the middle of the night so I'm off again. Take care of mother and the boys and the rabbit and Reino and the trees, and I'll be back as quick as I can."

His father leaned down to give him a rough kiss, poking him the way he had done when Joey was small and they rough-housed on the floor.

"Rory! You'll miss the plane if we don't start!" Mrs. Larkin stepped onto the porch. "I'm squeezing Jock in for the ride. I like company coming back."

"I'll bring you something that fits this time, old man," Mr. Larkin promised. "Just don't grow an inch anywhere. Anything you'd particularly like from Iceland?"

So his father was going to Iceland — without him. Joey wasn't even going to get as far as the airport.

"Oh, just bring me some whale blubber. That will fit." Joey tried to make it sound like a joke.

"Whale blubber for Joey. Bottled hot-spring water for Jock and surprises for Jerry and Ruth. Well, take care!"

Joey pulled his head down into the sleeping bag, cutting out the world as effectively as a turtle. There went the whole glorious conspiracy of a trip with his father. He wouldn't have cared if it had been a trip to the inside of a boiler factory in Weehawken, New Jersey, if he could have spent two weeks with his father. But his father didn't remember. He hadn't even said, "Look, this is too bad it's so sudden. If you had your passport, I'd take you along. We'll be prepared next time." He'd just forgotten.

Joey wouldn't cry even as a small boy. Instead he

suffered so intensely that he could hardly swallow because of the painful tightening in his throat. He lay
there now, feeling as if he hurt all over. When he
finally stuck his head out of the bag for some air, it
was still foggy. There was nothing to get up for, so
he fell back into uneasy sleep.

It was Reino who woke him next time. "Jerry says
your pa's off again. So I'm taking the rifle and going to
blast that red squirrel's eating the trees. Just thought
I'd tell you I'll be sitting up there somewhere with a
gun so you won't come crashing through on those big
feet and get shot for a moose. All right?"

"All right." Joey yawned.

"If you can't think of anything else to do, you could
hoe that corn," Reino told him. "Take good care of it
and it'll be just right to feast your pa when he comes
back in two weeks."

"I'm not going to be around today," Joey decided
suddenly. "It's a good day for fishing. So I'm going
cunnering."

"Good. What you don't eat I'll use for fertilizer."
Reino grinned, settling his cap more comfortably over
his seamed face. "How's the rabbit?"

Joey leaned over and unwrapped the box. It gave
him such pride to see Blitzen's ears rise up and his
whiskers quiver at the sudden light and noise. The
tiny nose wriggled.

"Hold out your hand." Joey picked the rabbit

up tenderly and put him in Reino's huge palm.

"He doesn't weigh enough to tickle. But you've done a good job, Joe. Made him look like a real rabbit at last. You want me to put him back in the swamp — near his brothers? Let him go back to his own life?"

"After sitting up nights with him? Never! He's mine. He's going to be my pet rabbit and ride in my pocket or my bike bag when he's bigger — and go everywhere with me. Put him down. Let's see if he'll hop."

The rabbit perched on the grass rug, looking as if he didn't have any idea of what to do with himself. Then like a wind-up toy, he took a little jump — and another — and another.

"He looks so pleased!" Joey lay down on the floor and watched the rabbit springing up and down.

"Well, I got other things to do beside watch a rabbit being a rabbit." Reino left. Joey took his time catching Blitzen, and feeding him, and then feeding himself. Then he looked for his hand lines, hooks and sinkers.

It was mid-morning before he left his bike in a tangle of wild roses and sumac trees at the edge of the road. He followed a path through tough grass to the rocks. It was low tide. He put his knapsack on a flat rock, checked the rabbit in his shirt pocket and sat down to bait hooks. The fog warmed up with the sun sulking just behind it.

Joey brought five hand lines on reels. After he baited the hook, he made sure the sinker near it was tied on tight. Then he unrolled about twenty feet of line and left it lying loosely on the rock. Taking just two feet at the hook end, he swung it quickly around and around till he had enough momentum to throw the line out. It spun over the water and plopped into the ocean about ten feet away, where brown seaweed washed up and down. The cunners, almost the same colors as the seaweed, poked about in the shallows. Joey soon had all five lines thrown out and sat down where he could watch them. He took off his low sneakers. The rocks, tide-cleaned an hour ago, felt cool. Patches of old whitened barnacles scraped his skin, but the blackened rock surfaces were extremely slippery. He moved quickly but carefully to tend the lines. Soon five cunners flapped in the pail.

Then a sea gull — big, gray and arrogant— slammed onto the surface and grabbed a cunner which had just hooked itself onto a line.

When Joey saw the line flying up in the air he made a dash for the reel and snatched it just in time. He played out all the line. What a crazy feeling — to be flying a live sea gull instead of a kite!

Just as the gull realized the fish was somehow attached to something trailing through the air, and dropped the fish from his beak, Joey slipped on the slimy rock. Before he could catch himself, he slid into several feet of water where a soppy mess of sea-weed broke his fall. Remembering the rabbit in his pocket, he turned so one shoulder hit the water first. But when he scrambled up, he was soaked.

So was the rabbit. A bait can, lead sinkers and harsh nylon line didn't offer much in the way of warmth. Joey finally placed the rabbit just inside the knapsack, which lay open on a rock. He spread his shirt out to dry, hoping the sun would soon shove the fog away.

It was a good day for cunners. Every few minutes one bit, so he was quite busy. When he remembered to check the rabbit, some fifteen minutes later, it was gone.

"It couldn't have hopped out of that knapsack and down that rock!" Joey argued.

But somehow it had. He ran up and down, stooping to look under rocks and poking through the tangles of poison ivy and beach pea vines and bayberry bushes. He searched through seaweed in the tide pools.

How could such a tiny creature — perhaps not yet ready to nibble grass and green plants — survive? Had it taken refuge under a rock where the tide would sweep in and flush it into a rush of waves? Or where it would be defenseless against the swift pounce of a water rat, or the weasels that scavenged the rocks? Or the owls who searched at night? Joey felt like a murderer.

He searched for about an hour and when he still

found no trace of the rabbit, he gave up. For a time he sat in deep dejection, feeling as if he should keep some kind of faithful vigil — waiting. Then he decided it was useless and the longer he sat there, the worse he felt. He cleared his lines of cunners, packed his knapsack and hurried away.

Mrs. Larkin was in the kitchen. "Enough cunners for a chowder?"

"I don't know. I'll give them to Reino for fertilizer."

"Too lazy to clean them? Or something bothering you?"

"I lost my rabbit on the rocks."

"What on earth did you take him down there for?"

"I just had him with me. He's been living in my pocket and he was there when I went."

"I *am* sorry. Raising animals just doesn't seem to be one of this family's successful ventures." She ruffled his hair. "Why don't you throw yourself into developing something that can't die or run away? How about learning to play the guitar, or the accordion? Or starting a nursery bed of pine seedlings for your father? Or studying seaweeds? Or taking up photography? Develop and print your own pictures?"

"Mum — I'm just not musical and smart like Jerry. And I'm not scientific and smart like Jock."

"You just think you're not. You won't even try."

They stared at each other, because they were back

46

again at an old and sore argument. Then they both said at once, "If Dad were here — "

Mrs. Larkin realized how forlorn he looked and put her hand briefly on his shoulder, because it embarrassed him to be hugged. "Dad told me he wanted to take you with him to Iceland. He planned to do all the red tape — passports and shots and all — next week. He was really disappointed that he couldn't postpone the trip until you could go with him."

"Then why didn't he tell me that?"

"Because he expected you'd understand anyway. He never likes to stand around saying he's sorry or apologizing."

"No, he doesn't. Well, I'll go see if Reino's knocked off the red squirrel."

He heard the chain saw down in the swamp. When he reached it, Reino had stopped for a mug-up. He offered Joey some coffee from his thermos.

"No thanks. I should have let you bring Blitzen up here after all. I lost him down on the rocks."

Reino considered Joey's sad face. "Look at it this way — maybe he wanted to lose you. Maybe he wanted to run away and see the world. There's no wild animal yet that wants to be caged and petted. Maybe fed and petted and get lots of attention. But not caged. Not someone's little slave animal."

"How do you know?"

"If wild animals didn't want to be wild, they'd have

overrun us people and piled into our houses years ago. Maybe we'd be in the cages."

"Maybe there'd be tigers running busses and lions directing traffic. And the Mayor would be a fox — "

They went on thinking up silly possibilities, until Joey's sorrow over the rabbit shrank a little. Reino was the one person around to whom Joey really talked — silly or serious. Reino was steady and Joey felt he could count on him. It was some time before Joey remembered about the red squirrel.

"Shot him right between the eyes," Reino said proudly. "And sat there till I got his wife, too. She came busy bodying along to see what happened to him — why he was late home with the lunch — and I plunked her, too."

"Well, which is better? To be wild, but caged and taken care of — safe from hunters and traps and other animals — or to be wild and free and get killed?" Joey wondered.

"I figure nature designed animals to be independent and fend for themselves. It's when men go interfering with animals there's trouble."

"But can't you be friends with a wild thing? Can't you get it to be friends with you — and not spoil it or take away its freedom?"

Reino shrugged his shoulders. "You'll have to find a wild animal and try."

"I know. It's what I want to do more than anything

48

else. But I'm just not good at things the way Jerry and Jock and my father are. I always flub them up somehow."

"What you need is a dose of good old Finnish *sisu*," Reino decided.

"What's that? Some evil-tasting medicine?"

"No, sir! In plain English it comes down to something like guts. It's more like built-in never-give-up-ever guts. As a matter of fact, you make me cross, Mr. Joey Larkin. You can work just as hard as your brothers and you could be as big a man as your father in your own way. You don't even try."

Those same words — twice in one afternoon! Joey's temper boiled up in him. He looked at Reino with spirit flashing out of his eyes.

"Good!" said Reino. "I made you mad. Punch me. Go chop some wood. Go build a bridge over the brook. Get good and mad and go do something. But do a *good* something. Not an I'm-mad-so-I'll-break-something."

Joey didn't know what to say, except, "I'll see you later."

He ran through the woods for a while, working off steam, and when he came out to the pond, he was ready to sit down and think.

He sat for some time before he realized there was a noise he'd never heard before. It was a shrill sound — a sort of whirring shriek, frantic and frightened.

Then he saw a small dark thing caught on the slippery steepness of a boulder at the far edge of the pond. It looked about the size of a box turtle, but it was moving much faster. And no turtle would be scrabbling or screeching like that, trying to climb up a rock, only to lose hold and fall back to a little shelf above the water. There it would turn and turn about, only to find itself trapped between the dark water of the pond and the harsh rock above.

What a funny noise it made! It was as shrill as an alarm clock and just as insistent.

Joey ran around the pond and climbed out on the rock. When he knelt down he saw the distinct markings of a baby raccoon.

He reached for it, and the creature snarled and hissed and showed its sharp white teeth.

But as soon as he took his hand away, it began its pitiful cry for help and tried again to scramble up the rock.

"Don't go away!" Joey told it. "I'll be right back to save you."

3

"COME HELP ME catch a raccoon!" Joey shouted, dashing into the house.

But no one answered. His mother and Jock were out and the only sound was Jerry's piano.

"Oh, Murgatroyd!" Joey muttered in disgust. "No one's ever here when I need them." He delved through the winter-storage closet, flinging things out behind him until he found his leather ski gloves. Running through the kitchen he grabbed the first cagey-looking object — a wide-mouthed wire basket for washing salad things, which lay flat until the handle

51

was pulled up. In the garage he found a small wooden crate. When Lancelot bounded out the door, he called him back and shut him in.

As he ran toward the pond, he hoped the raccoon hadn't climbed up and run away. Then he heard its cry, higher pitched and more frantic than ever.

He put the gloves and basket in the crate, stripped off his T-shirt and blue jeans and eased into the pond. He swam slowly, pushing the crate ahead of him. Near the rock he floated the crate and quickly pulled on the gloves.

The rock shelf holding the raccoon was several feet above his head and he slowly moved the crate up beside it. He couldn't see what was happening, and from the scrabbling and crying, it sounded as if the coon was even more frightened by the box. He could tread water for a long time, but in a few minutes his arms began to ache. How could he coax the coon into the box?

Then it happened. The coon, in his rushing back and forth, scurried off the rock and landed in the box anyway. The creature dashed about screeching, his toenails scraping against the wood, as Joey slowly lowered the box. Then he swam with one hand, hoping the coon wouldn't climb over the side before he reached the shore. The glove soon felt as heavy as a boxing glove.

Joey found a foothold on the shallow side of the

pond and walked out with the box. "Stop your yelling," he told the raccoon. "I'm only trying to help and you keep screaming like a burglar alarm."

But when he tried to pick the raccoon up, the baby lowered its head right down to the bottom of the box, arched its back, bared its teeth and hissed.

"Oh, come now!" Joey kept talking softly. "I'm not going to hurt you. I know I should let you out now where your mama might find you. But suppose your family's moved? Or you ran away? Besides you came along just in time to replace Blitzen. So you just stop being a noisy old baby and I'll take you home."

As he watched, the coon stopped on top of the wire salad basket. Joey grabbed the handle, the basket opened up and there was the baby coon, as caged as a bird, and so frightened that he didn't screech for a whole minute.

Since his sharp little claws stuck out through the wires, Joey carried the basket well away from his 'body. He ran right to the clothesyard in back of the house and tied the basket to one of the lines.

Then he went into the garage storage room and pulled out the huge wire cage he and Jerry had made for Gidney the Guinea Pig. It was still in good shape. Joey added the wooden box for a shelter, and a log for climbing and sharpening claws on. But what did a baby raccoon eat?

He knew the big raccoons who raided garbage pails

53

enjoyed everything from melon rinds to turkey bones. A clever pair of coons played outwitting games with his mother for one whole winter. She finally won by suspending the garbage pail on a rope out of their reach. Then Mr. Larkin came home from Bengal so full of enthusiasm about stalking tigers that he dismissed the raccoon-garbage problem with one sentence. "How utterly domestic! Buy a garbage disposal for the sink and beat them to it."

Joey knew, too, that Reino detested raccoons because they loved fresh corn. They stripped the ears and ate right down the cobs more neatly than any human. "I see any coons around here, I'll pop 'em," Reino promised every summer.

But this baby was too small to open garbage cans and cut down corn. He was so small, so furious and so intriguing. His eyes were small and startlingly black, with barely any white showing around the pupil. They were flat and staring, rather than round and rolling like a dog's eyeball. Bands of black fur, the badge of all raccoons, led from around each eye out to the edge of his small pointed face. His nose was as black as his eyes. The smooth close fur over the back of his paws was silver-gray, while the pads were black.

Joey brought a dish of milk. Then he broke up some old bread and spread it on another dish in the cage. He was ready to transfer the coon to the cage when

Reino returned from the woods, hot and cross, because with the gun and the chain saw and his lunch box he'd had too much to carry.

"What you got there!" he exclaimed. "Not one of those garden-tramping corn-eating pests!" Reino scowled as if he would load the gun with pleasure.

"Don't get mad at him, Reino. He's only a baby. And he's scared silly."

"He may be a cute little thing now, but do you know how big he'll get? Fifteen or twenty pounds. With a bite as powerful as a steam shovel. Raccoons can eat right through the side of a house, you know."

"You're kidding!" Joey turned the basket about, so he could admire the baby from all angles. "He's cuter than any kitten or even a puppy. What's a good name for a coon?"

"Trouble." Reino stamped into the house to put away the gun.

When he came out, Joey was trying to tumble the coon gently into the cage. But the baby held on to the basket so tightly Joey couldn't shake him loose.

"His hand is just like a human hand — the way he uses it."

"You bet," Reino muttered. "They can open anything and once they start opening things the only way you can stop them is shoot them. If your pa was here now — "

"He'd be just as curious as I am about a raccoon."
Joey was sure of that much. His father had an overwhelming curiosity about everything.

"If he was here now, I'd speak up," Reino went on.
"I'd tell him to tell you to put that thing right back in
the woods — right now. Or you and everyone else
will be real sorry later on."

"What's the trouble?" Mrs. Larkin came from the
garage. Jock raced after her. "What have you found
now, Joel?"

Joey pulled the basket out of the cage so she could
have a good look.

"A little raccoon — isn't he darling!" She put out
her hand to pat him.

"Don't touch him. He'll scratch. He's afraid of us."

Jock squatted by the cage. "He has five rings on
his tail. That disproves that story."

"What story?"

"A raccoon has a ring for each year like a tree. How
old do you think he is?"

Reino cleared his throat. "Maybe ten or twelve
weeks old. Mrs. Larkin, you shouldn't let Joey keep
him."

"One little raccoon?" She was surprised. "When
he's been longing for a wild pet?"

"They're scavengers and pests." Reino wore his
most unbending expression.

"I know those coons gave me a hard time about the

garbage pail. But this one would be so well fed he wouldn't have to go scavenger hunting."

"Mum — please can I keep him?"

"I don't see why you can't keep him until Dad comes home. It's only two weeks and then he can decide. Besides, if you put that baby out in the woods alone, what would he eat?"

"Fish and berries," Jock said.

"Mrs. Larkin, if you keep him two weeks you'll never get rid of him," Reino warned. "It's now or never."

Mrs. Larkin looked at Joel, once more holding the basket up so they all could see. The coon stopped screeching in terror, but he made whirring complaints.

"He sounds like a loose fan belt!" Joey decided.

Mrs. Larkin saw the delight and wonder on Joel's face. "You can keep him, on the understanding that if Dad says no any time, you'll let him go."

"Good!"

Joey laid the basket on the floor of the cage, deciding to let the coon disentangle himself and crawl out when he was ready. Reino's English failed him. He muttered something cross-sounding in Finnish and huffed off.

"The way Reino acts you'd think we'd adopted a lemming and he was going to invite all his friends!" Joey exclaimed.

"If you had a little tiger or a lion, I could see his

concern," Mrs. Larkin said. "But this is only a raccoon."

"He sounded as if he thought one raccoon could chew down a whole house," laughed Jock. "He's crazy."

They turned to look at the big buildings behind them. Nearest stood the three-car garage and large storage room which held the Graveley tractor, the power mower Joey rode to cut the lawns, the bikes, skis and all the varied paraphernalia of an active family in the country. Then there was a high-roofed handsome stone building, which was originally a studio built by an artist who worked with stained glass. It contained a large two-storied room of stone and great clear glass windows, against which some striking designs in stained glass still hung. Now it was the Music Room, where Jerry's grand piano was in almost constant use.

When Mr. Larkin bought the place, he connected the Music Room to the main house with a glass-enclosed stone terrace which Mrs. Larkin used as a green house.

Beyond was the kitchen wing and dining room, library, the screened porch, a large living room and a bedroom wing for Mr. and Mrs. Larkin, and two large bedrooms and bath, which the boys shared.

Looking at the solid lines of stone and glass and cedar shingles, and then at the ridiculous size of one baby raccoon, they burst out laughing.

"We can always barricade ourselves in the Music Room if he attacks," said Joey. "You wouldn't do that, would you, Coon!" He hung over the cage crooning. Finally the coon dared to leave the basket and pick his way across to the dish of food. He circled around it, snuffling and whirring. He stood in the milk dish and puddled his front paws up and down in it, spilling most of it. But he didn't try drinking it. He stepped on the bread and smelled it, but he didn't try eating it.

"According to my animal book," said Jock, "he ought to pick up the bread and wash it before he eats it. It should be instinctive."

Joey brought a bowl of water. The coon upset it. Jock helpfully refilled it from the hose. But the baby kept on whirring his complaints and walking around in the food.

"Maybe he needs his mother to teach him," Joey worried.

"You poor hungry baby," cooed Mrs. Larkin, hanging over the cage. "Try the nice bread like a good little boy."

"Mummy!" groaned Jock. "If you could hear yourself. Ick!"

"You'll be telling him to have a good din-din in a minute," Joey laughed.

"Go ahead. Ridicule your aged mother. But any mother can tell when a baby's hungry. Joel, I think we should buy some plastic baby bottles."

"Okay. Bottles will be a lot easier than feeding with an eyedropper."

But when Joey reached in the cage, holding out the bottle, the coon charged it. He rushed toward it, spitting, trying to frighten such an odd enemy. When the enemy didn't retreat, the raccoon lowered his head and arched himself into a corner.

"Oh, Murgatroyd! I just can't reach that far. Get the fire tongs out of the Music Room, will you, Jock?"

Jock brought not only the tongs, but Jerry, curious enough to interrupt his practicing.

"Joel, see if you can squeeze some milk out on his nose," Mrs. Larkin suggested. "Maybe he needs to smell it and taste it."

Joey squeezed the bottle, and a fine stream of milk hit the raccoon in the eye. The baby backed up again, screeching.

"Great!" Joey muttered. He stuck the bottle between the ends of the fire tongs and aimed at the coon, who was backed into the farthest corner. He finally put the nipple right on the end of the coon's nose.

Snap and gulp! The baby moved fast as a mouse trap. With one lunge he grabbed the nipple and tugged at it. After a while Joey's arms ached.

"Maybe he's younger than Reino thought, if he'll still take a bottle," Joey wondered. "Oops! Here comes Lancelot. Now what's going to happen!"

60

"Maybe he'll think Lancelot is his mother," Jock said.

"Lancelot is too jealous," Joey worried. "Do you think he'd kill him on sight if he weren't in the cage?" Lancelot was nosing the wire and sniffing, but the baby was still too preoccupied with his bottle to notice.

"You'll just have to keep the coon in the cage all the time," said Mrs. Larkin.

"Then he won't be much of a pet," Joey objected. "I'll teach Lancelot not to bother him."

"How?" Jock asked. "Lancelot's never learned anything but meal time."

"Meal time! That's my cue," sighed Mrs. Larkin. "I was going to suggest a picnic. But I suppose you don't want to go off now, Joel?"

"No."

Jock was disappointed. "You'll make us all stay-at-home coon-sitters, just like you tried to make us rabbit-sitters."

"No one scolds you when you won't leave some experiment. We didn't see the fireworks on Fourth of July this year because you were cooking something chemical and Mum wouldn't leave you home alone with it. And it didn't even blow up so we could have a spectacular in our own yard."

"I'll go fetch some submarine sandwiches and we can picnic at home," Jerry suggested.

"Good idea," Mrs. Larkin agreed.

Jerry took Jock with him. Joey was so completely absorbed in the coon that he was surprised to find his mother still watching. "Isn't he fun?" Joey asked as he fastened the cage carefully.

"I was watching you more than him," Mrs. Larkin admitted. "When something interests you, you really put your heart into it. I just wish there were more things that interested you."

That made Joey cross. Why did his mother have to turn his concern for the coon into an accusation about his lack of concern for what she always termed worthwhile things?

"Mum, a lot of things concern me. But you don't recognize them as real interests, because *you* never think about them."

"What do you mean?"

"Remember when you and Jock and I were playing Twenty Questions and I was thinking of something? You and Jock guessed all kinds of categories — art and music and science and goverment and foreign capitals and theater. You know, all that stuff. And I said no — none of them. And you got all unstrung because you said there couldn't possibly be any other categories?"

"I remember. It's my blind spot. You were thinking about sports."

"See? You keep trying to fit me into your idea. The kind of world you like — all your categories. But I don't fit. And Dad goes striding around all over the world, and because he's such a built-in success, he doesn't understand how anyone can *not* be successful at everything. I found a Christmas card you wrote to some friend, and on it you said I was a normal average boy. But you made it sound as if I was a disappointment to the whole family."

"Oh, dear!" Mrs. Larkin was shocked. "Where did you ever come across that?"

"It was in a wastebasket from the Music Room, and you said yourself you hadn't had a good clean in there since Thanksgiving because Jerry was so fussy about people stumbling around. I know I shouldn't have read it, if that's what bothers you."

"That isn't what bothers me as much as the fact that you and I don't seem to understand each other, Joel. That's sad. With Jock and Jerry, I can talk things out somehow. But you and I — well, maybe you're right. Maybe I haven't tried to see the value in the things you value. But maybe you haven't tried very hard to find values in what interests the rest of us. Things work both ways. Anyway, if you'll try, I'll try."

"Mum, what do you think I should do?" Joey's frown made Mrs. Larkin hope he was taking her words about new interests seriously. But he went on, "Should I take a run through the woods by the pond and just see if I spot any raccoons? His family, you know."

Mrs. Larkin laughed. "I never understood why persistence is supposed to be an admirable quality, but a one-track mind isn't! If you're even the slightest bit conscience-stricken about taking in a stray raccoon, run and look."

Joey pounded along, making so much noise that any self-preserving raccoon who heard him coming would scurry up the nearest tree.

He circled the pond and stopped in the thick underbrush where the coon might have lived. But there wasn't a hollow tree or any obvious burrow in sight.

He listened, but all he heard was the grumpy frog who ruled the pond and the knife-sharp shrill of a cicada. There were no rustlings in the thick summer leaves, nor furtive searchings in the underbrush, nor any mother animal anxiously calling.

Joey returned, his conscience smothered because he had at least looked, but very thankful he had found nothing.

They picnicked on the porch, with Jerry's portable hi-fi stereo providing concert music.

"Don't you ever like just plain quiet?" Joey complained. "I mean — don't you ever relax and let your ears rest?"

"I can. But then my head feels kind of empty," Jerry admitted.

"That proves my theory," Jock announced. "Some people stuff their heads with sound so they don't have to think."

"So the quality of your mind would depend on what you stuffed it with?" suggested Jerry.

"Sure. If you fill it with Beethoven—" Jock began.

"Just turn it down enough so I can think up a name for my raccoon," Joey begged.

"Am I looking forward to that Conservatory!" said Jerry. "If everyone else is music-minded, I won't have to worry about too much music. You know, it's hard trying to work all by myself at something."

"You've certainly never had any competition around here," admitted Joey. "When you play something, we all say 'That's great!' But come to think of it, I've never heard anyone else even try the same stuff. Anyway, what kind of a name fits a raccoon?"

"Something Wind-in-the-Willows-y?" asked Mrs. Larkin. "Like—Raccoon?"

"No, that's too cold."

"Did you see if the coon is a male or a female?" asked Jock.

"A male."

"With a mask," said Jock. "How about Bandit or Robber?"

"A name like that would make Reino hate him for sure."

"He's silvery and he's cute and he's black," mused Mrs. Larkin. "How about Sylvester C. Black?"

"How about an Indian-type name that describes

him?" Jerry asked. "Like Clever Paws?"

"Here Clever Paws! Here Clever Paws!" Joey tried it. "No thanks."

"You're always saying Oh, Murgatroyd. Why don't you call him Murgatroyd?" Jock asked.

"No. Murgatroyd is my all-purpose word. I'll just keep trying names till one fits."

That night the coon's shrilling woke Joey when it was still black dark outside. The kitchen clock said three, when he pried his eyes open enough for a good look. He filled the bottle and shuffled out to the cage. His flashlight beam picked up two red dots. Then the shape of the coon's head filled in behind the glowing eyes. But this time the coon didn't spit and hiss quite so long, as the bottle and tongs came near him. Nor did he back as far into a corner. He drained the bottle quickly. Joey yawned back to his hammock.

Awakened again at six by the creature's insistent crying, Joey was ready to name him either Hungry or Noisy.

That was the pattern of the next three busy days and interrupted nights. Joey finally moved the cage right outside the screened porch, so he didn't have to trudge at night.

"He should get used to our voices anyway," Joey decided. "Maybe half his yelling is because he wants someone to talk to."

"A raccoon is a nocturnal animal," Jock said. "He'd

much rather prowl around and discuss things at night."

"Why don't you name him Nocturne?" suggested Jerry. "That's a great name for a raccoon."

"It's better for a piece of music."

Reino referred to the animal each morning as That Pest. "Haven't you got rid of That Pest yet? You just wait till he chews his way out of that cage and into that vegetable garden. He'll start running for his life then — and I'll be chasing him."

But Joey noticed that Reino made a special trip by the cage not only in the morning, but also as he left each afternoon. He hunkered down to stare in at the baby, and sometimes it was three or four minutes before he'd straighten up again.

"Know thine enemy," growled Reino. But Joey was sure he saw a grin lurking behind the purposely ferocious scowl.

Still searching for a name, Joey settled down in the library with the Encyclopædia Britannica and looked up raccoons. He took some notes, and at the supper table he rapped for attention.

"Lady and gentlemen," he began. "My lecture this evening is entitled More About Raccoons Than You'll Ever Need to Know."

"Hear! Hear!" Mrs. Larkin encouraged him.

"The raccoon is a carnivorous beast, belonging to the large family called *Canoid*, which includes dogs, bears and raccoons. A subdivision of this family, *Canidae*, includes dogs, wolves and foxes. Something to do with their intestines and their teeth makes them different from the subdivision *Ursidae*, which is all the bears. Then there are the *Procyonidae*, and guess what they include besides raccoons?"

"Skunks?" asked Jock.

"Nothing as common as that. They include those big pandas from Tibet and China. And kinkajous from South America. How's that for a glamorous category?"

"Did it say how big they grow?" asked Mrs. Larkin.

"It says," and Joey quoted, "the typical raccoon, *Procyon lotor*, is a thickly built animal about three feet long — "

"Oh, help!" Mrs. Larkin looked horrified.

"Don't interrupt!" Joey was enjoying his rare opportunity to hold forth. "Three feet long, of which the tail is ten inches. Raccoons are found over the whole of the United States, in southern Canada and southward into Mexico. I found what they like to eat. But I didn't find anything that makes a good name."

"What do they eat? He's not going to enjoy a bottle much longer," Mrs. Larkin worried.

"A raccoon is an omnivorous carnivorous," Jock chanted.

Joey consulted his list. "They eat mice, small birds, birds' eggs, turtles — "

"You mean they can crunch right through a turtle shell?" Jock was fascinated with that.

"They don't eat the shells any more than we eat clam shells. They just sort of fish around inside and haul out parts of turtle, I guess. And they eat turtle eggs and frogs, fish, crayfish, insects, nuts, corn and poultry. I will now conclude my lecture. The raccoon is a good swimmer. It hibernates during the severest part of winter — "

"Good!" said Mrs. Larkin. "Here's to the snows of yesteryear. May they surround us this winter."

"We don't want to hibernate, too, Mum!" Jock protested.

"And may I say in conclusion," Joey raised his voice, "that the raccoon lives high up in the hollow of a large tree. The mother bears four to six babies at one time and keeps them with her about a year. Thank you for your kind attention and I hope that these few words will help you to enjoy and protect that great American institution — the raccoon."

"Congratulations, Professor Larkin, on a fine lecture," said his mother. She would have liked to add, "and for taking the time to look something up in the Encyclopædia for a change."

But Joey was halfway out the door.

"And now Bungling Bros. Circus presents Joey the Wild Coon-Tamer and His Famous and Intrepid Act — Bottling the Baby. Where's my gloves?"

"If you were a real tamer," Jock teased, "you'd go into the cage with just your bare hands and a water pistol. But you wear a football helmet, and your hockey-shin guards and your skin-diving flippers — "

"I do not, and since I can't find my gloves, I'll go in unprotected."

Mrs. Larkin started to say, "Don't." But she knew how much Jock's teasing bothered Joey. It was time to let him work things out his own way.

"You stay here, Jock," Joey ordered. "I don't want little old Coony all upset and he doesn't like your smell. You must be a very peculiar smeller, because he always wrinkles his nose at you."

"Smell! I don't smell. Mummy, he called me a smeller."

Joey disappeared. He disliked verbal entanglements with Jock as much as he would have welcomed hand-to-hand combat with him.

Through the open kitchen door they could hear the coon's excited screeching as Joey approached his cage. They heard the hinged top creak and Joey say, "I hope the bottom of the cage is strong enough because I'm coming in with you. And I'm going to pat you whether you like it or not."

Mrs. Larkin stood still with a dirty dish in her hand, listening.

"What's the matter?" Jerry came in to pick up the car keys. "Do you think one baby raccoon is out there stamping on Joey's chest and chewing him to death?"

"Hardly. But I do worry about animals and bites."

70

"Then you better make Joey get rid of him now, because most puppies and kittens nip and scratch. And so will this fella. I'll be home by midnight."

But Jerry came dashing back. "You really ought to look at Joey."

Mrs. Larkin and Jock rushed out. There was Joey crouched in the cage, his long legs very much in the way. But the coon lay on his back, propped like a baby against Joey's arm, while Joey held the bottle. As they watched, the coon's small hands found the bottle and clutched it, too.

"How did you ever manage that?" asked Mrs. Larkin.

"Easy. I decided all the noise he made was more fear than threat. And I'm bigger than he is. So I just grabbed him and turned him over and stuck the bottle down the throat. See?"

Joey picked up the coon's paw and the coon curled it around his finger. "He's not fierce at all really. And you should feel the pads on his back feet. They're as soft as the palm of a baby's hand. You wouldn't think anything wild could be so soft." Joey ran a finger down the coon's head. His gray plushy ears twitched. "Want to see something funny? See — his ears are lined up so they aim frontwards — right off the top of his head."

Joey scratched the side of the coon's head and one ear swiveled around till it was at right angles to its for-

71

mer position. "He can move his ears around like a radar-dish."

When the bottle was empty, Joey held the coon up. His body was about the same size as Joey's rather large hands. Joey stuck his finger into the coon's mouth and rubbed it over the tiny gleaming teeth.

"Mum, you don't need to be afraid of his biting. Look — he's biting now and I don't even feel it. They're just silly little baby teeth."

"I think it would be wonderful if some Fairy Godmother would wave a wand and put a spell on him so he'd stay that size forever," said Mrs. Larkin.

"Fairy Godmother — hooey!" said Joey. "What you need is a mad scientist with a spray-on can of Instant No-Grow. Maybe I'll call him Cuddly, although his fur is funny. It's sort of springy and tough."

"What was Pooh's real name?" asked Mrs. Larkin. "Wasn't it something gentlemanly like Edward T. Bear? How about R. A. Coon?"

"But he shouldn't have a cute name," decided Joey. "Because he's real. He's not an animal in a story like Pooh. He's my real raccoon and he's beginning to feel like somebody to me. He feels like either Robert, Albert or Andrew."

"Why?" asked Jock.

"I don't know."

"Maybe you're getting a message by E.S.P."

"What's that?"

72

"Extra-sensory perception. A sixth sense."

"That's as good a way to find a name as any other," said Mrs. Larkin. "Which will it be? Robbie? Bertie? Andy?"

"Robbie is too much like Robber. Andy. Handy Andy. No — that's not coony enough. He's Albert. Good old Bertie. What's the matter? Don't you like it, Mum?"

"Somehow it's a name I associate with mischief and hi-jinks. Maybe it's because of Bertie Wooster in the P. G. Wodehouse stories. Luckily it will be months before he can climb out of that cage. And of course if Dad says we shouldn't keep him, that's it."

"He'll love Bertie. Wait and see."

Once Joey discovered that Bertie was touchable, he spent hours playing with him. They rolled about in the grass together. Bertie invented games, sneaking up on Joey and pouncing suddenly so he could lick Joey's ear. He liked to play with Joey's longish straight blond hair. He would lean on Joey's head and pat the hair and sift it through his paws.

"First-class massage!" Joey claimed.

"I hope he keeps those claws out of your eyes," worried Mrs. Larkin.

"Oh, Mum! He's not scratching. He's playing. Did I tell you he likes raisins now?"

"No. But I notice that hamburg for lunch is half gone. Are you responsible for that?"

"Partly. I gave it to Lancelot."

"Whatever for?"

"Lancelot has jealous fits when I play with Bertie. And I don't want Lancelot to eat Bertie up in one gobble. So this morning when I took Bertie out, I gave Lancelot some hamburg. Just to make him feel good. I tried some on Bertie, too, and he loves it."

"I'm glad raccoons don't grow as big as horses." Mrs. Larkin shut the refrigerator door with a sigh. She noticed three empty plastic bottles by the sink. "You ought to give those bottles a good scouring. They smell sour."

"Bertie's graduated. He drinks out of a dish now. But I haven't seen him dunk his hamburg or raisins in water yet."

"Maybe you have to show him how to wash his food."

"I did. I put some raisins in his water dish. And he pats all around and stands on them and picks them up and drops them back and steps on them again. He'll eat one or two, but then he'll go over and eat dry ones off the other dish. Maybe he's not a true raccoon."

"It could be because he's out of his element," lectured Jock. "He may be confused because these are hardly the same conditions as his native habitat."

"I know that. I wish I could find a hollow tree big enough."

"You wouldn't need much of a hollow for him now."

"For both of us." Joey glared at Jock.

Joey was easy to find during those days. He was often in the cage, where he took a cushion and a radio. Or on the lawn nearby. When he first put Bertie out on the grass, he used an old tie around his neck for a soft strong leash. But Bertie made no attempt to run away.

The next problem was to keep Lancelot from grabbing Bertie and shaking him to death or to keep Bertie from annoying Lancelot and provoking an attack. Despite Mrs. Larkin's worries, Joey insisted on putting Bertie on the grass and then calling Lancelot to come and lie down. Joey sat between the two animals, stroking the dog's head and holding Bertie far enough away so he couldn't poke the dog.

"Now you just have to be friends," Joey would keep talking quietly. "Because we all live here and I expect Bertie to be in and out of the house. You'll just have to get along with each other. Understand?"

Joey gave the animals this pep talk at least twice a day.

Lancelot obviously did not enjoy the attention the small animal received, but he was a good dog and didn't attack the raccoon. He disdained and ignored him, and began to act like an overgrown puppy to claim attention for himself. He rushed at people and flung himself against them and wouldn't move till he was petted. He began sleeping on couches and chewing pencils and sofa cushions.

Mrs. Larkin stalked around chasing Lancelot off furniture with a rolled-up newspaper. "You big clumsy oaf. Don't you know man is still your best friend? We haven't deserted you. It's all in your mind."

If Lancelot came crashing by when Bertie was out of the cage, or some strange person stopped to talk, Bertie dashed for Joey's feet and climbed up his legs. Joey soon wore blue jeans instead of shorts, even on the hottest days, as Bertie's small but sharp claws left a network of nicks on bare skin.

At first Jock complained that Joey wouldn't let him play with Bertie. But after Bertie had nipped his ear rather hard and suddenly scrambled down Jock's back and a long expanse of bare leg, he didn't care so much about handling him. He went back to his tropical fish, insisting, "They're a lot more affectionate and a lot less trouble."

"I don't know why everyone claims Bertie is a lot of trouble," said Joey at lunch, after spending a lazy morning playing with the coon. "He's great fun and you're all jealous."

"He's too much fun. Have you looked at the calendar?" asked Mrs. Larkin. "See the big gold star drawn around tomorrow? That's the day Dad hopes to fly back from Iceland."

"So?"

"Look at the uncut grass and the unweeded garden. You've done nothing but play with that creature for two long weeks."

"Why should I be the only one ever to cut the grass and weed the garden?" Joey felt stubborn. "Jerry and Jock have been doing just as they like and you don't chew them out."

"But Jerry had to practice."

"All day? Every day? For what — a special concert? Or just on general principles? He hasn't lifted a finger to help anywhere. I don't think it's fair. And what about Jock?"

"He's too little to run the power mower," said Mrs. Larkin. "And you're the only one who knows which are weeds and which are plants."

"Because Jock and Jerry won't bother to learn. Because you think what they want to do is more important than lawns and gardens. So you excuse them and it all lands on me. Just for a change I have a project. It's raising a raccoon, and it's as important to me as playing scales is to Jerry, or building a robot is to Jock. Maybe more — because it involves something that's alive. Someone who depends on me."

"Dad and I depend on you."

"Not really. You just decided I was the one in the family who needed character and chores would be character-building. So I got them all."

"That's not true. Jock bikes to the mailbox for us and picks up the mail every day. He sets the table and helps me clear it."

"Baby jobs."

"At least I do them without being reminded all the time," said Jock.

"And Jerry keeps his room clean," Mrs. Larkin added.

"That's just so I can find things in a hurry, because I hate to waste time on nothings. Mum, Joey is right. I haven't done anything but indulge myself in music since I was accepted at the Conservatory. It isn't fair to organized households. I'll run the mower this afternoon. What needs most help in the garden?"

"The carrots. About a thousand of them came up all at once. They need thinning."

"Show Jock how to do it. He does get away with doing mighty little, Mum."

"Are you sure you know how to run that machine, Jerry?"

"You just sit on it and drive it around."

"And keep your fingers out of the machinery," said Joey. "If an idiot like me can run it, you can run it without even thinking about it."

"What are you going to do, Joey?" asked Jock.

"Take Bertie up a tree with me and watch you all work." But first Joey took the mower out for Jerry, who had run it once when it was new, just for fun, but admitted he'd forgotten how it worked. Joey explained what to do and not to do.

Then he showed Jock the three rows of carrots to be thinned and how many plants to leave in the rows. With a pitchfork he loosened up a long row of earth. "Stick the biggest ones you pull up in there and throw the rest on the compost heap."

"But I'm not sure which are the carrots," complained Jock.

"Oh, yes, you are," said Joey. "If you can build all kinds of model this-and-thats from diagrams, you can diagram your way through that mess. Get going."

He climbed a favorite cherry tree with Bertie. But the coon was too lively. He wouldn't stay still on his shoulder and kept scurrying off on a branch and then screaming for help when it grew too small and swayed underneath him. So Joey swung down and lay under the tree, growing drowsier and drowsier. From the woods Reino's chain saw gave sharp-pitched screeches in spasms of noise that shrieked and then died. The power mower sounded like the drone of bagpipes — fading off at the far end of the lawn.

But the air felt empty, until Joey realized he missed the sound of Jerry's piano, which usually blended all the sounds into music. Now they were just noises — drowsy noises — not sounds. He woke himself up suddenly, realizing that Bertie was loose and could wander off anywhere if he didn't watch him.

But Bertie was right there. He lay curled up by the curve of Joey's shoulder. His bright eyes flashed when Joey lifted his head, and he put a paw out to touch Joey's arm. "Good boy!" said Joey, putting his large hand over the tiny paw. "Have a nap."

Joey woke from a confused dream in which his father had returned from Iceland and brought him dozens of pairs of sealskin boots — all too large. Joey kept saying, "Wait! Wait! I can fill them." But he couldn't.

The sun edging beyond the tree hit him full force. He was sweating and uncomfortable and suddenly aware of a voice yelling, "Joey! Joey! Help! Come quick."

He jumped up, not sure which direction the cry came from. "Hello! Yell again — "

"Near the brook — "

It was Jerry's voice, but strange and faint. The whirr of the mower was silent.

Joey ran. Jock saw him dash and chased after him.

When Joey saw Jerry bending over in pain, he ran faster. He reached Jerry in time to catch him as he fainted. Then he saw blood and realized Jerry was clutching his right hand.

"Jock — turn around! Get Mum to drive the station wagon right down here. We've got to get Jerry to the hospital quick!"

80

4

JOEY RIPPED OFF his T-shirt and wiped at Jerry's hand.
Then he saw that the top of Jerry's index finger was
hanging by a scrap of skin, but the top of the middle
finger was gone. Vanished! It was a raw ugly sight,
and despite the fact he was sweating, icy shivers raced
over him.

He tore a wide strip from the T-shirt. Then he tried
to push Jerry's index finger back together and wrap
it as tightly as he could.

Jerry's life was music, and eight fingers weren't

enough. Joey thought he was going to be sick. But when Jerry's eyes opened, full of fear, Joey promised him desperately, "Everything will be all right."

With relief he heard the station wagon coming. Mum drove right through a border of cutting flowers.

"Jock is phoning Dr. Harvey to meet us at the hospital. Come on, Jerry, you can make it to the car!"

Between them, they half-carried and half-pushed Jerry and slid him into the back seat.

"Mum — hold Jerry's hand up — just like this — for a minute," Joey urged. He turned and knelt in the grass. A whirling blade could knock a rock farther than a ball player's home run. What would it do to a fingertip!

"For heaven's sake, hurry up, Joel! He's bleeding badly."

"Mum — don't panic. Just give me thirty seconds. It's vital."

As he talked, Joey scanned the grass. He couldn't give up. He was the one who could not panic. He had to find it. Then he saw it. He dashed to the car, grabbed the Kleenex out of the glove compartment, wrapped up the fingertip, and stuck it in his pants pocket.

"Okay, Mum. I'll hold his hand up now. Let's go."

They bounced over the lawn, along the narrow road, which wound through the woods for a mile and a half before it reached the main road. "If we just don't get stuck behind a snail-type summer tourist where we can't pass!" His own hand was now as blood-covered as Jerry's.

"We'll make it all right," said Mrs. Larkin grimly. "We'll make it."

In a few minutes more she drove up to the emergency entrance. Dr. Harvey, their family doctor, was waiting with a stretcher and a nurse. But Jerry managed to walk in.

"You look fine," grinned Dr. Harvey. "From what Jock said I expected to see Jerry walk in here saying, 'Look, Doc, no hands.'"

Joey hastily handed the Kleenex to Dr. Harvey. "Here — you'll need this."

Dr. Harvey, flashing a look of sudden understanding, stopped joking and took Jerry quickly through the heavy swinging doors.

"Are you the boy's mother?" asked a nurse. "Would you go in the office and fill out the forms, please?"

Mrs. Larkin took a deep breath and walked slowly into the office. Joey's knees felt as wishy-washy as seaweed and he collapsed on a bench. He could not turn off the insistence in his mind that this was his fault. If only he had cut the lawn when he was supposed to, instead of playing for days with his raccoon. Jerry had given up so many things he enjoyed, like baseball, because his hands might be injured. And then when he took over Joey's job —

x

83

The ache in Joey's throat almost strangled him.

"Is anyone helping you?" A nurse bent over him.

"Oh!" Joey gasped. "I'm all right. It's my brother who had the accident." Then he looked at himself and realized he was clad only in blue jeans, and his hands and chest were blood-stained. He found a washroom and scrubbed himself clean. When his mother returned, he was sitting on a bench, shivering.

She touched Joey's shoulder and her hand was as cold as he felt. But she said, "Go outside and run around to get warm."

Joey couldn't seem to move. "I'm sorry. If I'd done my job, Jerry wouldn't have been hurt. It's all my fault."

"That's what seems obvious, doesn't it, Joel?"

His heart sank. His mother, of course, would be all sympathy and concern for Jerry. He could admit his guilty feeling, but he wanted forgiveness and understanding even so.

Then his mother went on, looking him right in the eye. "But you mustn't blame yourself. Jerry could just as easily have mowed all summer with no accident. I'm sure the accident happened not because he was on the mower instead of you, but because his mind wasn't on the job he was doing."

"And I told him it was a job he could do without thinking about it," Joey moaned.

"It's happened. Placing blame is a luxury we don't

need. Now run out and get warm. You're all goose pimples."

"Thanks, Mum." He fled. He ran around and around the parking lot until his goose pimples disappeared. As he passed their car, he saw an old sweat shirt in the back and pulled it on.

He waited inside with his mother for an hour until Dr. Harvey came out. "Congratulations to the one who had presence of mind enough to bring in that fingertip. Was that you, Joe?"

"You mean — the tip of Jerry's finger was cut off?" Mrs. Larkin turned white.

"Didn't Joe tell you?"

"I knew he was looking for something, but I just didn't reason it out. I was too concerned with Jerry's bleeding."

"And Joey was smart not to tell you in front of Jerry. That's good thinking in an emergency, fellow. Now don't worry, Ruth. The top of the finger was cut off almost to the first knuckle. But there's every chance his fingers will be as good as new. I've sewed it back on."

"Good enough for playing the piano — the way he plays?" Joey asked anxiously.

"Yes. I'm going to keep him here for a day or two, because he had a severe shock and lost a lot of blood and he's exhausted. But I'm sure he will come out of it just fine."

On the way home Joey groaned. "Oh, Murgatroyd! Bertie was out of his cage. He's probably run away by now."

"And I wonder what's happened to Jock. I never like to leave him home alone in case he decides to experiment with something. He may have blown himself up by now."

Joey found the cage open and no Bertie in it. He searched all the way around the house and through the garden without seeing a sign of one small raccoon. Jock lay reading in the hammock on the porch.

"I know we left in a tearing rush. But couldn't you at least have stuck Bertie in the cage so he wouldn't run away?"

"You know Bertie always scratches me. He's your raccoon and you always say he doesn't like my smell."

"That's just because I wanted him to be mine and nobody else's. But in an emergency like this, you could have taken care of him for me."

"Next time, with your permission, I will." Jock calmly turned a page.

Joey stamped out and searched again. He whistled up Lancelot. "You can come, boy. Bertie usually rushed up me like a tree whenever you're around. Up a tree! Maybe he went up and can't get down!"

Joey was staring up so hard that he walked right into the back of Reino, who stood looking at the vegetable garden.

They both grunted at the impact. "Where's your eyes anyway?" asked Reino. "This garden looks as if you'd weeded it with your eyes shut."

"Jock managed that," Joey explained. "For a kid who can build all kinds of junk with sets of stuff, he sure unbuilt those carrots."

"It looks like he weeded by the handful and jumped up and down on the rest."

"Oh, Murgatroyd!" said Joey sadly. "Jock just helped me into a bigger ness, and Jerry helped me out and now he's in the hospital."

He explained the day's events to Reino. "And will you help me look for Bertie? Jock won't bother and Mum's kind of unstrung."

"Me look for That Pest? You need your head examined."

But Joey looked so stricken that Reino changed his mind. "All right. So I need my head examined."

Around and around they went. Reino said, "Maybe he went back to the pond where you found him. That might be his home territory."

But as Joey started toward the pond, Reino called out, "Here he is!"

He pointed to a large empty flower pot. Bertie, curled into a ball, slept soundly in his refuge. When Joey lifted him out and put him on his shoulder, Bertie yawned extravagantly. Then sleepily he began searching down inside the neck of Joey's sweat shirt, patting his paws up and down. It tickled and Joey laughed happily.

"You didn't run away! Isn't that great, Reino?"

Reino put out his tough hand and Bertie sniffed at it. Then Bertie took the hand in his front paws and felt it all over — staring thoughtfully at Reino.

"He's cute all right, Joey. I can see why you want to keep him for a pet. But I'd better not make real friends with him."

"Why not?"

"Because you may need someone who doesn't love him too much some day."

"I can teach him to be good. I'm sure I can."

"Then good luck to you." But Reino took his hand away gently. "You're a picture," he sighed, looking at the boy and the coon together. "You're some picture."

"And you're a tough old Finn," teased Joey. "Real tough."

Two days later Mrs. Larkin brought Jerry home early in the afternoon. Both Jock and Joey rushed to see what they could do for him.

"Thanks, fellas, but I'm not helpless," Jerry grinned. "I'm supposed to rest and not to worry. So I'm going to read and talk on the phone a lot and catch up with my friends. And Joey if you need a coon-sitter now and then, I'll sit."

Joey grinned.

"Jock, you can invent something so I can play cards

with one hand — the sooner the better." That sent Jock off, full of ideas.

"Listen, Joey, Mum says you blame yourself about the accident and I want to tell you, *don't*. It was my fault because I wasn't thinking about what I was doing. When something caught under the mower, I did turn it off. But I just didn't wait until the blade had stopped revolving, and I stuck my hand in too soon. And Doc Harvey told me how you saved my finger. So I want to thank you, Joey — and tell you maybe this was all baked in the fortune cookies. I was getting to be nothing but a fanatic about music and using it as an excuse for everything. So stop looking like Son of Doom and smile."

"Okay. Any time you want Bertie for company, just tell me."

His heart lightened by Jerry's understanding, Joey rushed around the yard and the garden. By the time his father called from the airport late that afternoon, everything was in fine shape.

Two hours later when Mr. Larkin strode in the front door, he announced, "I'm taking a vacation. Absolutely no jobs. Not for one whole month. It's time we all stay together and do things together. How about it? Jerry's not tied to his piano. Shall we all see America first in a tent? Fly to a dude ranch for three weeks? Take a windjammer cruise?"

"Aren't you tired of traveling, dear?" asked

Mrs. Larkin. "What would *you* like to do most?"

"Sit right down and not move an inch," admitted Mr. Larkin, falling into a large chair. "But as long as I'm at home that front office always thinks I'm interruptable. How's that for a word? Interruptable. It's the story of my life. Wouldn't you like to go away, Ruth? You never have a chance to travel."

"I seldom have a chance to be home with you for a whole month. That would be an adventure."

"What about you, Jerry? Wouldn't a change of scene keep you from wanting to worry those piano keys?"

"Not really. I'll be away all next winter and so will my whole gang. Off to college in all directions. I'd like to see as much of them as I can now."

"We tried camping two years ago," Jock reminded his father. "All we saw was rain and too many other campers."

"I wouldn't want to go anywhere unless I could take my raccoon," Joey said. "You've got to come and see him, Dad — right now!"

"You know, I don't think I can rise out of this chair," groaned Mr. Larkin. "Couldn't you bring the raccoon in to see me?"

Joey looked questioningly at his mother. So far she had refused to let the animal in the house, insisting, "Bertie should be strictly an outdoor pet." But she could see Joey's impatience to show off his pride and joy, and her husband so rarely gave in to fatigue. "All right," she compromised. "Just this once."

So in came Bertie. Mr. Larkin admired him with enthusiasm, patting him and tickling him, and rolling him about on the rug. "What a find, Joey! What a gorgeous animal a raccoon is! Look at those bright eyes — he's not going to miss a thing, is he?"

And Bertie didn't miss a thing. He charged the fringed border of the upholstered couch. He lay on his back and pulled himself in and out, batting the fringe as he disappeared under the couch — only to shoot out somewhere else seconds later. While Mrs. Larkin went to the kitchen to make cold drinks, Bertie became bolder. He rushed up and down and over the back and arms of the couch like an eager mountain climber. His tail floated triumphantly behind him as he leaped and jumped. He flew across tabletops. But when he tried to climb up the fragile greenery of the potted plants, Joey grabbed him.

"Naughty!" said Joey and spanked him.

Bertie's fur was so thick that a spank didn't even tickle. He sensed that he was the star of the evening's entertainment and frantically wiggled from Joey's grasp.

He did acrobatics on the rungs of wooden chairs. He discovered his tail — and tried to ignore it. He held treasure hunts in every crack and crevice he could sneak his busy paws into. He streaked across the room and rushed up Mr. Larkin's trouser leg and into his lap. He pried into his jacket pockets, feeling the loose coins as if he were a bus driver solemnly finding the right change. When he tried to get a paw into Mr. Larkin's trouser pockets, it tickled and Mr. Larkin rose — sliding Bertie onto the floor with a bump.

Bertie lay on his back and suddenly put his paws over his eyes as if he were very tired. When Mrs. Larkin returned with the tray she found four males all hanging over one small raccoon and talking to him as if he were a baby.

"Out with him, Joey!" said Mrs. Larkin, noting the wild disorder of the tabletops. "Out, out, out!"

"Oh, Ruth," said Mr. Larkin. "I haven't had such a good relaxed laugh in ages. He's not doing any harm."

"Not now he isn't," she agreed. "But Reino says — "

"Reino carries on a feud with anything that isn't human. He says deer eat the young trees and red squirrels and pine grosbeaks eat the new growth on the old trees. Woodchucks and rabbits chew the garden and skunks dig up the bulbs. Moles undermine the lawn. What does he claim the raccoon does, besides rattle garbage pails?"

"He says they chew down houses," Jock shrilled.

Joey picked up Bertie. "If I want to make a good pet out of him, then I shouldn't let him run wild through the house. I'll take him out."

The next evening Jerry's fingers pained him constantly. Dr. Harvey came by and said he was sure there was no infection. "Even though you *say* you're not worrying, Jerry, you are. We know playing the piano means everything to you now. Nerves are funny things. I can give you some pills for the pain, but the biggest help would be not to worry, not to think about your fingers at all."

So the Larkins tried to help. They attempted Monopoly, but Jerry was the first one to lose all his money. Jock played chess with him, which was mind-consuming, but took so long over his moves that Jerry became impatient. When he began pacing the floor, Mrs. Larkin said, "Joel, we all need a good laugh. Do you want to let that foolish animal in — just once more?"

Bertie provided complete diversion. He turned the living room into the giddiest of fairgrounds. The straight chair with the ladder back became his jungle gym, the rocking chair his merry-go-round, the darkness under the couch his spook house, from which he kept emerging upside-down in astonishment. Before the Larkins knew it, a whole hour slipped by in which they had done nothing but enjoy Bertie's antics.

The next evening Mr. and Mrs. Larkin went out, and when Jerry became restless and too conscious of his throbbing fingers, he said, "Joey, please bring Bertie in. Mum wouldn't mind, I guess."

The three boys lay on the floor and let Bertie explore them. He was always solemn about pockets, looking dreamily but expectantly off into space while his paws felt everything carefully. Jock soon gave up. He didn't enjoy the light scritch-scratch of the coon's claws, and Bertie made too many nips and darts at his glasses. But Jerry and Joey found marbles for Bertie to roll and chase, and an old toy wind-up car that kept the raccoon intrigued for a long time.

When the boys finally turned on the TV, Bertie climbed up between them on the couch. But he kept worrying Joey's hand with his teeth.

"Doesn't he ever give up and go to sleep — like a puppy or a kitten?" asked Jerry.

"If I put him in his cage, he'll sleep for a while. But this must be his wildness. He never seems to rest when I'm with him."

By the end of the week, Bertie was the established evening entertainment. Mrs. Larkin complained about his claws and his habits. She made Joey clean up after him and hopefully they put newspapers down for Bertie to use. But she would break off a complaint to laugh and say, "Look at that nut now! Oh, dear, I waste so much time just standing around watching him."

That evening she was dashing around the kitchen in bare feet, trying not to step on Bertie. But she didn't see that Jock had given him an ice cube to play with. So when Bertie came and stood on her bare feet with his ice-cold paws, she screeched and threw a panful of peas all over the room. Bertie loved that, as rolling, chasing and eating the peas made a great game for him.

Gradually Jerry's fingers hurt less and he spent evenings with his friends. Jock embarked on an astronomy project that kept him outdoors with a telescope and charts of the heavens all evening. Mr. and Mrs. Larkin were entertaining or being entertained almost every night.

So Joey's companion was Bertie. If Joey caged him, so he could weed the garden or mow the lawn without interference, Bertie crawled up the wire sides, screaming with rage at being neglected. When he was out of the cage, the raccoon stuck so close that Joey took him for walks in the woods with no fear that he would run away.

Bertie dashed up and down tree trunks and explored underbrush beside the paths. If Joey called him, and he was investigating something, patting it over with his usual thoroughness, he might not come at once. But if Joey impatiently walked off, Bertie would waddle-hump after him as fast as he could.

Reino, meeting them among the rows of red pines, shook his head. "That animal would have a hard time if he suddenly had to go back to the wild. You've got him so he acts just like any old dog or cat."

But Reino changed his mind when he knelt by an outside faucet at the house, cleaning a large fish. He no sooner cut it open than Bertie rushed through Reino's legs and dove into the fish. He dragged out the intestines with his teeth while his front paws scrabbled for the liver.

Reino started to grab for the liver, too, and Bertie growled. He arched his back, his fur rose up, but he stayed his ground, one foot on the fish. Even though his growl was more a squeal because his mouth was full, he meant business.

"Did you say he was too tame?" asked Joey.

"I take it back. I hope that's the last time any raccoon goes diving through my legs and into a fish. Wow!"

Near the end of Mr. Larkin's vacation, he suggested they take a three-day camping trip through the White Mountains.

"I know Jerry needs to go away from the house and the sight of that piano. His fingers are itchy."

"What would I do about Bertie?" asked Joey.

"Reino can feed him and let him run once in a while," Mr. Larkin decreed.

With his quick organization, Mr. Larkin made everyone pack his gear and loaded the car that night. "We will start at seven-thirty sharp tomorrow."

Joey woke at six. There was something about the eager calling of the birds, the leaves stirring exuberantly in the morning breeze, which excited him. He could hardly wait to see the mountains, even though it meant missing Bertie. He decided to get up and give Bertie a good run before they left.

96

Bertie strolled out of the box in the cage, yawning. "You poor mixed-up raccoon. You play days and sleep nights. Your whole normal life is turned around. What are you going to do about it, huh? Huh?"

Bertie put his paw solemnly in Joey's outstretched hand. Then he licked the hand.

"Want to climb a tree with me? I'll give you a head start."

Joey put the coon on his shoulder and Bertie took his favorite stance, his own head bobbing above Joey's. They climbed the cherry tree. Joey stopped in a comfortable crotch about twenty feet up. Bertie scrambled on.

"Bertie!" warned Joey. "You're heavier than you used to be. Those branches aren't big enough for you."

Just then a bird lit on a twig. Curiosity or greed — Joey wondered which — sent Bertie scurrying toward it. The slim branch suddenly bent, and since Bertie was more interested in the bird than the tree, he unexpectedly lost his grip. With a squeal of surprise, Bertie flew through the air and there wasn't a limb between him and the ground.

He plunged straight down the whole twenty-five feet and hit the grass with a horrid "thwump."

Joey's heart seemed to leap as Bertie had! He stared down at the ground. Bertie didn't move at all.

"Joe! Breakfast! This expedition gets under way

in exactly thirty-seven minutes — "

Mr. Larkin's eager call reached Joey as he knelt by Bertie's breathless body.

"Dad — " Joey's voice rose and cracked. "I think Bertie's dead!"

Mr. Larkin bounded from the porch and squatted by Joey.

"He fell from almost the top of the tree." Joey stroked the coon's head, but there was no responding quiver.

Mr. Larkin picked up a paw and let it go. It fell limply.

"He's not breathing at all," Joe worried.

"If he's dead that solves the problem of taking care of him while we're gone," said Mr. Larkin practically. Then he saw the horror reflected in Joey's eyes. "I didn't mean to sound so tough about it. It's a shame. He made you a very interesting pet."

Joey just stood there.

"Come in and eat, son. Time's a-wasting."

"I'm not hungry."

"You will be, and I don't intend to stop on the road until we hit the White Mountains. There's Reino. I'll tell him to take care of this — among other things."

Mr. Larkin called Reino into the house for coffee and a check list of duties.

Stubbornly Joey sat down by Bertie. He had failed again. He had lost his rabbit and killed his raccoon.

98

And he still secretly berated himself for giving Jerry's accident the chance to happen. Why was it that everything he cared about involved tragedy?

"Your father says for you to hurry, Joe." The hand on his shoulder was Reino's. "You go on. Don't worry about this."

But as Joey looked, he saw a shudder run over Bertie's body, as if an earthquake were shaking him. Bertie's mouth opened and he gasped for air. Then one ear twitched.

"Reino! He's not dead! He just had the wind knocked out of him. Boy, isn't he tough! Isn't he wonderful!"

Joey's face glowed with delight, and then concern. Bertie moved his paws, he rolled onto his stomach and slowly pushed himself up. Then he coughed and choked. The choking shook his whole body until at last he coughed up what must have been his breakfast and a great deal of blood.

"Reino — what will I do? He's really hurt."

"Looks that way."

"Joe!" called Mr. Larkin in a stern voice. "If you don't come right now, you can't have anything to eat before we go."

"Reino, are you going home nights or will you be staying here at the house?"

"Your mother wants me to stay in case of fire. So she's fixed up Jerry's room for me."

"Could I stay with you? I can't go off and leave Bertie now."

Bertie was lying down again, his breath coming hard, his eyes a little glazed.

"It might be better if you went, Joe," Reino told him gently. "It would be easier than sitting here and watching him, if he dies."

Joey shook his head. "I'll be right back. Just stay with him for a minute — please."

Mr. Larkin stood in the kitchen issuing brisk orders. "Clean up that plate first, Joe."

"I'm not going. Bertie isn't dead. He's just badly hurt."

"But Joe!" Mrs. Larkin turned in dismay from the sink.

"Of course he's going," said Mr. Larkin. "This is a family expedition, Joey boy, and we need you. All for one and one for all, as the saying goes."

"Joel, you can't stay here alone with a sick raccoon."

"Reino will be here. He and I both know how to fry eggs and make sandwiches. Please, Mum — "

Mr. Larkin threw up his hands impatiently. "If that animal dies an hour after we leave, you'll have three long days of meditation and wishing you'd come with us. But if you are a sentimental humanitarian — or animalitarian or something — instead of a spirited adventurer, you're stuck with it."

Mrs. Larkin watched Joel's face. "I'm sorry about

Bertie. He's been great fun for us all. Are you *sure* you don't want to come?"

"I'm sure."

"All right then. Let me show you what's what in the refrigerator, so you and Reino won't starve completely."

She put her arm around him and talked about leftovers and package mixes and oven temperatures. Joey barely heard her. He saw his father leave the room in an atmosphere of disgust toward his sentimental son, and he was bewildered. He had expected sympathy and understanding and some support for his decision. But instead he felt his father was cross because Joey didn't appreciate this trip enough to go on it. And here was his mother, whom he'd expected to refuse, allowing him to stay.

"Mum, how come you didn't put up a fuss about my staying?"

"Because you wouldn't enjoy the trip if you worried about Bertie. Besides, I think it takes a spirited adventurer to nurse a raccoon back to health. Joel, I'll phone you tonight around seven — from somewhere. I hope everything goes well."

"Thanks, Mum."

He heard them go. Dad blew a tattoo on the station-wagon horn. His mother's voice floated out, "Goodby, dear!" He didn't know how long he sat, just watching Bertie gasp and shake. Every now and then Bertie

101

stretched out a paw and seemed to clutch at Joey's hand for comfort. The refreshing morning faded into bright uncomfortable noon. Joe was surprised when Reino brought a huge tuna fish sandwich and a mug of milk. Reino sat down and opened his lunch box.

"You better move into the shade. You're looking kind of cooked."

"I'll put up an umbrella. Reino, do you think my father's good at his job because everyone always does just what he says? Do you suppose anyone ever argues with him, or wants to do something differently?"

"Your father has a genius for figuring out where things go wrong and how to fix them. He doesn't believe in a lot of waste motions."

"Or in waste emotions, I guess."

"Well, he's good at persuading people that he's right — and that he knows the best and quickest way to do things," Reino added.

"But what if he isn't always right?" It was such a disloyal thought that Joey felt uncomfortable.

"He must be right ninety-eight per cent of the time, or his company wouldn't have been rushing him all over the world the last ten years."

Joey heard Reino's words with relief.

"But you know families don't run like businesses," Reino went on thoughtfully. "There's too many personalities in families, if you know what I mean."

"I sure do."

102

Joey brought the beach umbrella and a dish of milk and a spoon. Every now and then he spooned milk into Bertie. By mid-afternoon Bertie breathed normally and his eyes didn't look so fixed and staring. At four when Reino came back from the woods, Joey went into the kitchen and made up ice-cream sodas for both of them.

"I'd camp out tonight and put the tent right up over Bertie," said Joey. "But they took the tent. Can you help me move him onto the porch, Reino? I want to be right there if he needs me."

Reino found a piece of Masonite big enough for a raccoon-stretcher and carried Bertie to a safe spot under the hammock.

"He's all right for now, Joe. Lucky for you I do all my own cooking, because I can make you a real good supper if your mother has the right cans."

When Mrs. Larkin phoned from New Hampshire, Joey happily reported he was full. "We had baked beans mixed up with beef stew and soy sauce. You ought to try it. Now Reino's going to make a cake — "

"Please don't tell me what he's putting in it. Tell me about Bertie."

Joey gave her the details.

"Put a blanket over him in case it gets cold in the night," she advised. "Dad's honking outside the store here. We're going back and smoke some steak over our campfire. I'll call again tomorrow night."

Joey dozed restlessly. Whenever he woke, he reached under the hammock to assure himself that Bertie was there and still breathing. But after midnight a persistent rain fell, and its steady thrumming on the roof soothed him into such a deep sleep that Reino finally woke him.

"You expect me to stand around waiting your breakfast? It's going on nine o'clock already."

"It is!" Joey sat up in his sleeping bag. "Ha! I know you. If you say it's going on nine o'clock, I'll bet it's two minutes past eight. Right?"

"You know me pretty well then," Reino admitted. "You want ketchup and cheese on your fried eggs — or mustard and chopped parsley?"

"You really live, don't you! Is that why you never got married? Because you like such crazy things to eat that no woman would cook for you?"

"Don't you tease, Joe. Independence is a fine manly thing. So's my cooking."

Joe had to admit that the egg with cheese and ketchup was delicious. "Wonder if it's raining up at Mt. Washington. You know, I don't think Jerry wanted to go on this trip, or Jock, or Mum, either. But Dad did. So they went." Joey scratched his head. "When Father orders, I guess we all just march."

"But you don't do something your father orders because he orders it as an order," Reino argued with

104

him. "You do it because you love him and respect him and want to please him."

"Well," Joey chewed thoughtfully. "We all want to please him, that's for sure. Dad's been my hero for years. I guess that's why his getting cross because I wouldn't leave Bertie kind of shook me."

Joey watched the rain hurl itself gustily out of the sky. "I'll bet that porch is wetter than a tent, though." He moved his sleeping bag into Jock's room. Then he fixed up a cardboard box for Bertie, and put it on the kitchen floor. Reino sat at the table, fitting a new handle on an ax.

"Bertie's head is up and his ears are twitching. I think he's going to recover completely."

Late in the afternoon Bertie stood up in his box, shook himself and ate a rather sumptuous meal of bits and pieces from the refrigerator.

When Mrs. Larkin phoned, she sounded tired. "We'll be home tomorow night. It's cloudy and damp up here, but we climbed a lot today. Some wild raccoons found our grocery supply last night, and what brazen creatures! They just stood on the picnic table and defied us. They went off with a bag of hard candies, each one wrapped up in paper. This morning we found a whole pile of papers behind some trees. The two of them must have sat there unwrapping the candy and eating it and laughing at us for a long time. Bertie

105

is very sweet and well-behaved compared to those un-couth characters."

Joey explained that the weather was wretched and he'd moved into Jock's room and Bertie was better. "Mum, will you tell Dad I didn't mean to be ungrate-ful about the trip? It would have been great to go mountain climbing with him. Especially if he taught you about rock climbing and rappeling with a rope the way he promised."

"Oh, he did, he did!" groaned Mrs. Larkin. "I can still feel every inch of the lesson."

"Tell him I'm sorry I missed it. But the way Bertie's come through I still think it was right for me to take care of him."

"I'll tell him, dear. You know, Dad is so enthusiastic about doing things he doesn't always understand when everyone else isn't just as enthusiastic. I hope my air mattress doesn't leak again tonight."

Joey spent a completely happy evening. Wood crackled in the fireplace. "And no smoke in the eyes like a campfire," he commented. There was a wild suspense story on TV, followed by a far-out science fiction thing. Bertie lay on Joey's knees, warm and loving, rising to explore a pocket or to tug at the shiny zipper on Joey's blue jeans. Joey decided he'd better keep him from learning to unzip zippers! But the rac-coon didn't bounce and run as he usually did.

"Look at that. He's on his back and he'll let me

scratch his stomach," Joey told Reino. The old Finn in the next chair was half asleep and pulled himself up with a grunt.

"He sure trusts you, Joe. Well, you can sit here and watch this hypnotizing machine as long as you want, but I'm going to bed."

"You think I should leave Bertie in his box in the kitchen tonight? Or put him in his cage? Or take him with me in Jock's room?"

"It's still blowing and raining. His cage would be like sitting under a waterfall."

Joey placed the cardboard box next to his bed, and Bertie tramped around on his bit of blanket, poking at it like a fussy housekeeper, and at last settled down. It was nice to hear the lullaby of the fish tank again, going "glub-glub, ger-bubble, ger-plup." But after a while Joey pulled the blanket over his head to shut out the monotony of the rain and the insistence of the tank.

Much later something tickled him awake. Bertie was exploring Joey's head, scratching lightly through his hair and feeling his face.

"Take your busy hands off my nose," Joey muttered sleepily. "Go back in your box." He lay half awake while the raccoon climbed over him, diving to bite at a moving arm or knee under the blanket. "Bertie—this isn't playtime. Go to sleep."

Encouraged by Joey's voice, Bertie nipped at the

boy's ears. Finally Joey sat up, turned on the light and grabbed for the raccoon. "If you weren't sick, I'd spank you." Joey made him lie down in the box and tucked the blanket over him.

But nighttime was after all Bertie's true working day. The sleepier Joey became, the livelier the raccoon grew. He climbed back on the bed and held races with himself from one end to the other, using Joey's body for a hurdle. For a while Joey grunted, if Bertie surprised him too much, but finally he fell sound asleep despite the raccoon's activity.

When he woke the next morning, he saw Bertie asleep in the box. Then as he sat up and stretched, he looked about the room and groaned.

"Murgatroyd H. Jehosophat! How could one small raccoon do all that by himself!"

Joey took one step and his feet slid out from under him. He smashed onto the floor so hard that his head bounced and he lay there stunned. The crash brought Reino running all the way from the kitchen.

Reino slid, too, but he saved himself by sitting on the bed. "What happened in here?"

Groggily Joey sat up. "Bertie spent the night on a hunting and fishing trip. Look at Jock's tropical fish — all over the floor. Dead. Jock's going to kill me."

"Why do you suppose Bertie pulled them out of the tank and then didn't eat them?"

"He probably wanted someone to play with him,

108

and I wouldn't. Those fish must have flipped and flapped and kept him busy quite a while."

Reino found one half-eaten fish. "Maybe he didn't like the taste. These probably have a different flavor from brook and pond fishes."

Joey peered hopefully into the tank. "Where's Double-Bubble? Jock had one bug-eyed black something-or-other that smacked his lips just like a bubble-blower, and Jock loved him. I'll bet Bertie ate Double-Bubble. I don't see him anywhere."

"Are there any left in the tank?"

"Three stupid goldfish. The cheapest, most common ordinary kind. I suppose I'll have to buy him new fish. And I heard him boasting that he had forty dollars' worth of exotic fish. Forty dollars would be my allowance for nine whole months."

For the first time Joey stared at his raccoon, who slept calmly on, with something less than love.

"You better clear this room up before Della comes in to clean today," Reino warned him. "If she sees this, she might even quit on your ma."

"How could I have slept through it?" Joey wondered. Bertie's scampering over the crowded shelves had set off a mass of magazines and pamphlets which spread like a glacier over the floor.

Strewn among them were marbles from a box Bertie had opened, pieces of a balsa-wood airplane model which Jock was making, chewed and unchewed plastic

Indians from a Fort Apache set which had been dumped from its cardboard box. And to finish the horror, there was Double-Bubble's body among the remnants of a box of checkers. Joey groaned.

"A car just drove in," Reino said. "Della's husband must have brought her early today."

"She can do this room last. I'll get a mop and a shovel, I guess." Now Joey realized that both his ankle, which he'd twisted, and his head, which he'd banged, hurt. Slowly he got to his feet and stood there, trying to pull himself together.

Then to his horror he heard familiar voices. The campers were home early. Jock's eager feet dashed down the hall. Instinctively Joey picked up Bertie and protected him in his arms as Jock skipped in.

At first Jock's mouth opened, but no sound came out. Then as he saw all the dead fish, he screamed, "Vandals! Vandals! Everything's ruined."

5

MR. AND MRS. LARKIN and Jerry came running.
Joey tried to calm Bertie, who clung to Joey's head,
hissing at all the noise.

"Jock! Enough!" thundered Mr. Larkin. "Well,
Joe — is there a good reason for this havoc?"

"Two, sir." Joey looked his father right in the eye.
"Bertie recovered. I slept too hard to hear him."

"But you shouldn't have been in here with that
beast!" yelled Jock. "You killed all my lovely fish."

"Now, Jock," urged Mrs. Larkin. "Pull yourself together. Joey feels as badly as you do about it, I'm
sure."

"Worse. Because I'll have to buy him some fish. And you'll all blame Bertie. He'd barely moved out of his box for two whole days. He nearly died, you know. How did I know he'd snap back all at once like a yo-yo? Listen, Jock — he was sick and I was taking care of him. Like you took care of your fish when you had them in the bathtub with the Epsom salts — "

That was the wrong thing to bring up, as Jock gulped more noisily than ever.

"Look — no one yelled at Jock when he spent three days taking care of sick fish. You all said how lovely and scientific. Maybe you think I should have slept out in the cage with my raccoon and taken care of him out there in the wind and the rain — "

"No, I don't," said Mrs. Larkin. "No one should sleep in the wind and the rain. That's why we started home at five o'clock this morning. We were drenched."

But Joey was wound up and couldn't stop. "You can't blame Bertie. He was only being a raccoon. Just hunting. And fishing a little."

"Jock, stop snuffling and listen," Mr. Larkin ordered. "Joey certainly deserved a dry bed in the house. But it was not wise of him to include Bertie." Mr. Larkin went on analyzing the situation. "Especially when Joey couldn't wake up enough to cope with his friend's natural instincts. Now the problem is first, the loss of Jock's fish, and second, what to do about the raccoon."

"Make him pay for the fish and get rid of the raccoon," said Jock.

Joey turned pale. Reino said, "Excuse me. You don't need me," and left.

Joey felt deserted. Then he wondered if Reino wanted to leave before being asked leading questions, like "How tame can a raccoon get?" or "Can you stop a wild animal from being destructive?"

"I'll pay for the fish somehow," Joey promised. "But please don't make me get rid of Bertie. Don't you think it's as worthwhile for me to study a raccoon as for Jock to make lists of fish? He can buy his. I have to find mine."

"Do you have a scientific angle in mind?" asked Mr. Larkin a bit sarcastically.

That stung Joey. "I know you think I'm lazy and I'm not smart like the other boys," he burst out. "But I do like to find things out. And I'm finding out a lot about raccoons. And about people. I'm finding out how an untamed beast can affect a household that thinks it's very liberal and very scientific and very sophisticated."

"Wow!" said Mr. Larkin. "You surprise me. All right, Joe. You certainly can observe how a raccoon is affecting our household. Whatever kind of household you think it is. You pay Jock for any fish he bought himself. A lot of the exotic ones were presents, and since Jock is a fierce hinter, I wouldn't worry about his eventually restocking his tank. But from now on, Bertie spends the night in his cage."

Joey struggled with mopping and sorting out the room, and tried not to clobber Jock, who sat on the bed and supervised. Right after lunch Joey bolted.

"I'm taking Bertie off in the woods for the afternoon."

"Do your wandering while you can," his mother agreed. "Next week this time you'll be in school."

Joey made a sick face and groaned. "That will be rough on Bertie. Will you play with him while I'm in school, Mum?"

"Oh, Joel!" It was Mrs. Larkin's turn to make a face. "He always nips me if I pick him up. And it's a struggle to put him back in the cage. He'll just have to adjust to your school life, that's all."

The next week dazzled them with bright clear weather. Mr. Larkin and Reino cruised the tree farm, planning the winter's work. Joey hiked about, Bertie at his heels, sometimes joining the tours or spending a few hours cutting brush. But often he holed up in the green tower, with nothing on his mind but vague dreams. Even Bertie calmed down in that secret place and stretched lazily on the cool rock.

Once as Joey approached he glimpsed Jerry, sitting

still as a yogi. Joey started quietly off, but Bertie chirruped and gave them away.

"Come on in," called Jerry. "I'm saying goodby to
my youth." Then he laughed at himself before Joey
could snort at him. "That sounded stupid, didn't it?
But nothing can ever be the same again, once I go off
to New York."

"When is Dr. Harvey letting you play the piano
again?"

"I can start Monday, and build up by half an hour
each day. He says everything came out fine."

"You're lucky, knowing what you want to do. Or
didn't Dad keep stirring you up all the time over what
you were going to be?"

"He made lots of suggestions. Engineer. Doctor.
Lawyer."

"Always a real important career. I guess he thinks a
concert pianist is important enough so he'll let you do
it."

"I'd do it anyway whether he let me or not, because
so far I haven't thought of one other thing I'd rather
do. But it's up to me whether I can be a really important pianist or not. Why the questions? Something
bugging you?"

"Yes. I don't know what I want to do at all and
Dad's always at me. He says be a vet, or a biologist, or
a philosopher, or — "

115

"Look, Joey, Dad is a kind of overwhelming guy. I heard some men talking about him once. They said he was brilliant, but aggressive and even ruthless. It made me mad, until I saw those were qualities he needs in his work. But don't let him overwhelm *you*. He'll admire you if you stick up for yourself."

"But he didn't. When I wouldn't go on the trip, he was cross. That's what I don't understand."

"So he was disappointed. He really wanted your company. Hadn't you thought of that?"

"No. I just thought he didn't realize what was important to me. I still don't think he does."

"Well, what is important to you?"

"That's the horrible part! Jerry, I just don't know. Lots of things are important to me, but I guess they're not really important to anyone else. And the more Dad expects me to know what I want, the more confused I get."

Jerry sat, sympathetic and quiet, and waited while Joey struggled to explain himself and couldn't and gave up with a shrug.

"Maybe if I try sitting like a Yogi on this rock I can think better," Joey muttered.

"This hideout is all yours now. You've got three more years to hang around and enjoy it before you have to face the cruel world."

"I'd enjoy it a lot more if Dad wasn't always breathing down my neck, waiting for me to say, 'Aha, I'm going to be a mathematician or a computer-analyst.' If I say, 'Aha, I'm going to be a custodian senior grade or a sanitation engineer or a dump inspector' — all perfectly good jobs, you know — he doesn't think it's funny. Sometimes I think the only one around here who likes me just the way I am is Bertie. I don't know what I'd do without him."

Joey lay down on the rock and Bertie climbed onto his chest. He slid his agile paws into Joey's pocket.

"Sorry, Bertie — no raisins in the pocket any more. Mum says she is tired of washing them and they don't iron well."

"I'll miss old Bertie when I'm in New York," Jerry sighed. "I'll miss it all."

But once Jerry began practicing again, the time rushed by. First Mr. Larkin flew off to Turkey and then Mum drove Jerry to New York. Joey returned to school, starting his sophomore year with more misgivings than hopes. But he quickly fell into a routine of early rising and taking Bertie on a brisk walk before school. Then Bertie would settle down in his cage. Very often Joey even had to wake him up in the afternoon.

In other years Joey whisked off on his bike to wherever the boys congregated for touch football or soccer. This year he stayed home to play with Bertie.

"Why don't you ask the boys to come here?" asked his mother. "I don't want you to resign from the human race just because you have a raccoon to baby-sit."

Reino helped him nail a basketball hoop onto a big backboard and they put it up on an oak tree. Reino finally agreed that the grass on the lower lawn was tough enough to withstand scrimmage. Joey spread the word and, with Bertie as an extra added attraction, the Larkins' yard became a popular playground.

After Bertie nipped two players during a football roughhouse, he was banished to his cage. But whenever he saw Joey bounce the basketball over the lawn, Bertie ran for the oak tree.

He teased the boys by sitting on the hoop and chirruping. But as soon as they became impatient and tossed a ball up, Bertie scrambled into a crotch five feet above the board and net. There he would lie, head down, intently watching the ball.

"What a referee he'd make!"

"I'll bet he could blow a whistle, if we taught him," boasted Joey. But Bertie preferred to bite and rattle the shiny whistle Joey dug up for him, than try to blow it. Joey spent all his evenings with Bertie, until Mrs. Larkin complained.

"Joel, you're not putting enough time into homework. You rush through so you can let Bertie into the house and turn on the TV. Then you lie on the couch with him and watch that infernal blabber-eye for hours."

"But you said he couldn't come indoors unless I watched him. I can't watch him and do my homework. He spills paint and eats my pencils and messes up my papers. So I'm not really watching TV. I mean I've got it on for something to do while I'm watching Bertie."

"Huh!" said Mrs. Larkin. "Leave the TV off. Bertie makes a better program any night."

"You don't let me do anything," Joey grunted.

"I'm letting you keep Bertie, and I don't know whether that makes me an Extra Understanding Mother or a Compleat Nut."

At the end of October Mr. Larkin came home and, although he expected momentarily to be summoned to a job in Scotland, it was several weeks before the call came.

"This means I'll miss Thanksgiving," he mourned. "Maybe I'll be so busy I won't miss the day, but I'll miss being with you. Want to come with me this time, Joey boy, so I won't be all alone on the holiday?"

"You never took me up to see about a passport or shots or anything, Dad," Joey reminded him. "Remember? You just talked about it and then you went off suddenly. And you never mentioned it again. So I'm not ready. Besides, who'd take care of Bertie?"

Mr. Larkin flushed and quickly changed the subject. "Oh, yes, Bertie! Bertie, the gold-plated excuse. I've been meaning to talk with you about your life

119

as an animal-trainer. It's all-consuming, isn't it?"

"What do you mean?"

"I mean you've dropped out of everything. What happened to Scouts? You were all set to work for your Eagle, but you haven't even gone to a Scout meeting since I've been home."

Joey squirmed. "Bertie's in his cage all day while I'm in school and at night when I'm asleep. I have to spend afternoons and evenings with him. He'd get sick from not enough exercise and attention."

"Take the long-range view," said Mr. Larkin. "What will mean more to you later on? A few hours more spent with a raccoon or an Eagle Scout rating?"

"I don't think that's a fair question," Joey protested. "It isn't that clear a choice, is it? I may not have Bertie forever. I can always go back to Scouts some time."

"Our PTA finally organized square dances for the kids and Joel went once," Mrs. Larkin added. "Then he said he had to stay home with Bertie. Honestly, Joel — you're cutting yourself off from too many things you'll wish you'd done when it's too late."

"Jerry's crowd loves square dancing. Every Friday night. Routinesville. My crowd doesn't. We'd rather play our own records and catch up with whatever's the thing right now. I don't always like to do the same things Jerry did. *I'm me.*"

"That I know," sighed Mrs. Larkin.

"Joe," Mr. Larkin observed, "the point is this. Do

120

you have a pet **raccoon**? Or does a pet raccoon have you? And who is benefiting from the arrangement?"

"I am. He's mine and I love him and he loves me."

"It won't last. He's not really yours. He'll go back to the wild or if he doesn't we might have to give him to a zoo. And in the meantime you're missing all kinds of opportunities. **Scouts.** Square dancing. A trip to Scotland."

"Maybe," Joey said stubbornly. It stung him that his father talked about taking him on trips and then never took care of the necessary red tape so he could go. So he decided to stick up for himself. "I have a *feeling* — a kind of something I can't explain — that's going to last me all my life, long after Bertie's gone. And no square-dancing Scout on a trip to Scotland would even know what I'm talking about."

So Joey stayed home and missed organized activities and Mr. Larkin missed Thanksgiving. He phoned them and he sounded so lonely that Joey felt guilty. "Something is really jinxing this job," Mr. Larkin complained. "I hope I'll be through by Christmas. You'll all have grown so much I won't recognize you."

But the one who grew the most was Bertie. He tripled his size. His diet of dog food, raisins, crackers and milk agreed with him. His fur shone, the long silver hairs gleaming, while the stubbier brown or black hair bushed out until he looked very fat.

Bertie still didn't like to be patted. In fact his fur

121

was so tough and thick that the human hand never slipped over it easily. His fur felt more like a sponge made out of stiff wool — resilient but spiky. If he was wet, he smelt quite repulsive.

If anyone put a hand on him, Bertie's reaction was to throw off the hand. A light touch anywhere on his body would send him rolling about. Whenever Joey wanted to tease him, he'd touch the back of the coon's head and Bertie would immediately put his paws on top of his head, looking indignant and ridiculous.

His idea of play was to chew Joey's hands, not hard, but continually. Or to make little rushing attacks on his person, to catch a sleeve or a pant leg and tug at it. Joey's hands were always scarred from nicks and scratches and Mrs. Larkin worried until she finally consulted Dr. Harvey, who said Joey's last tetanus shot should still be enough to protect him. But she should continue to be observant and watchful.

"Oh, I am," Mrs. Larkin assured herself. But there were times when she found it difficult not to allow her concern for an unpredictable situation spoil Joey's good times with Bertie. When she found his jerseys and knit turtlenecks full of holes, she scolded, "Put on an old shirt before you roll around on the floor with Bertie. I just found one shirt that looks like a sieve."

But as Christmas approached Bertie presented them with a larger problem than ripped shirts. One morning Joey no sooner went out to the cage than he ran

122

in again. "Bertie's gone! He pushed the top open and he's wiggled out."

"How did he manage to open it? I thought you had nails bent over the wooden frame that holds the wire?"

"I do. But he's found out how to work the nails free. I can't leave food out for him. It would freeze. Where do you suppose he's gone?"

"Why don't you take Lancelot for a run? Maybe he could sniff out where Bertie might be holed up."

All fall Lancelot had been in a huff because of the attention given Bertie, but he never turned on him, even when Bertie trotted over and put his paws on Lancelot's fascinating tail. Lancelot would leap up, and if Bertie had a good grip he would sometimes sail right off the floor. But he never hung on for more than a second, and he never really attacked the dog. He was either curious or deliberately teasing. Lancelot was annoyed, but not very brave. Yet he was jealous enough to droop and develop a nervous eczema. So when Joey actually called Lancelot and took him out for a run, the dog raced and barked as if he'd suddenly turned crazy.

"A great help you are," Joey scolded him when Lancelot dashed after a squirrel. "You're supposed to stand still and sniff and then point in Bertie's direction, you idiot."

Joey called, "Bertie? Bertie?" That drove Lancelot

into more of a frenzy and he whirled about. "You'd scare anyone away, Lancelot. I'll take a quiet walk by myself after school."

But it was dark by the time Joey came home. Hopefully he looked in the cage. It was empty.

"Don't worry," Reino told him. "He's probably found a nice hollow tree that's cozier than a wooden box in a breezy cage."

"Every time I put rags or old cloth in his box, he takes them out. You know, the only time he wanted a blanket was when he was sick?"

"They're clean animals," Reino said. "He probably didn't want to fuss with housekeeping a lot of messy rags. I'll bet you he's right on the kitchen doorstep tonight at the time you'd bring him from the cage for supper."

Joey did his homework in the kitchen, so he wouldn't miss a scratch or a chirrup at the door. Eight o'clock was the time he usually fetched Bertie. When eight came and ticked by, Joey's heart sank. Something must have happened to the runaway raccoon.

Then at five minutes past eight, whang! Bertie's full weight banged against the aluminum storm door with a crash as effective as the cymbals in a band.

"He's back!" Joey opened the door joyfully.

Bertie stepped in, looking very pleased with himself. He did not bite Joey's outstretched hand. He licked it politely. But once the reunion was acknowledged, he ran to his dish. Without his morning food, he was hungrier than ever.

Joey tried caging him that night, fastening the lid carefully. The next morning, Bertie was out and off again, but returned for supper. This happened for a week. The raccoon accepted the cage each night, because he knew he could escape.

Finally the week before Christmas, Joey said, "I'm not going to bother even to put him in the cage. He's worked things out the way he likes them, so I'll go along with it."

After Bertie spent the evening wrestling amiably with Joey on the rug and then sitting on the couch as he watched television, Joey carried him to the back door. "All right. You're free! Go find your house. Good night."

He left Bertie loose on the back step, shut the door and snapped out the lights. He stood in the dark, trying to see in what direction the coon wandered. But it was a murky night. Bertie blended into the dark and disappeared.

The next morning the Larkins were surprised to find themselves in the midst of an early but thorough snowstorm. The driving, searching, sharp flakes stung and crawled into chinks and cracks.

"No school today!" Joey and Jock cheered.

Mrs. Larkin looked at the calendar and worried. Mr. Larkin had planned that date as his return from Scotland. Also Jerry should be arriving from New York for vacation. By suppertime they were all edgy, as it was still snowing.

"Must be a foot and a half deep out there!" Joey reported. "Do you suppose Bertie will wallow through this? Or stay in his hole?"

"Any animal would have sense enough to stay in his hole," muttered Mrs. Larkin. "It's the human beings who go wandering around in storms trying to get somewhere when they shouldn't. I wish Jerry would phone."

About eight o'clock the snow stopped and just blew about in unsettled gusts. Mrs. Larkin sat near the phone and Joey sat near the kitchen door. Finally at nine, the phone rang. Jerry said he'd been making up two exams he missed, and he'd start home in the morning. At ten Mr. Larkin phoned from New York, where his plane landed instead of Boston. Mrs. Larkin suggested he call Jerry and plan to travel together.

"I feel so limp I'm going to bed," Mrs. Larkin said. "Waiting for news seems more exhausting than traveling. Joel, Bertie must be all right. He's probably sound asleep in a nice cozy snow palace."

"He's hungry and I should have put him in the cage last night. He might not have tried to escape when he saw it was snowing."

"Not Bertie! He probably spent the first hour dancing around catching the flakes. Or tasting them. Or

126

stepping on them. I'm sure raccoons have lived through millions of snowstorms."

"Well, I won't feel right about letting him go at night until I see him again."

The next morning, a Saturday, flawless crystal snow glistened outside, unbroken by a single paw print. Joey rose early and was frying three eggs when Mrs. Larkin came in, yawning.

"I hope the plow comes before Dad and Jerry try to break open the road with their suitcases."

"Where do you want me to sleep while Jerry's home?"

"I'm glad you reminded me! It would really be easier for you to stay right in Jerry's room, and I'll make up a couch in the Music Room for him. Do you suppose Reino will try to hike up here today?"

"He's not supposed to come Saturdays. But he couldn't get here yesterday, and he has an old-fashioned idea about working five days a week if he gets paid for five days a week. So he'll probably show up."

"I wish that weren't called an old-fashioned idea. We need more people who faithfully do what they're supposed to, like Reino. We couldn't live here in the woods, with your father away so much, if Reino didn't cope with things. And you, Joel. You've been such a tremendous help to me this year. I want you to know that."

"Oh? I thought you thought all I did was eat more food and take up more space and outgrow more clothes. And watch raccoons."

"I don't always tell you what's in my head." She smiled at Joel. "But I want you to know how I feel before the travelers come bursting home full of noise and ideas."

Joey looked at her suspiciously, remembering several questions she'd asked recently about his marks, which were barely average, and his teachers. After one long airmail from Dad, she was unusually thoughtful. He'd look up to find her staring at him, as if by studying his face intently she could also penetrate his brain.

"Mum!" A chilling thought gripped him. "Does Dad have some horrible idea like sending me away to school? Because I won't go. I love it here. I can swim and skate right in my own backyard and there's all my friends. And Bertie. I couldn't leave!"

"You could swim and skate at most any school, and making new friends is a valuable experience. And Bertie isn't permanent — believe me."

"Dad did write about a school!" Joey felt as if he were turning to ice inside. His father, arriving full of enthusiasm with a scheme to brighten Joey's educational future, would be a formidable man to face.

"In a large public school like yours, with eighteen hundred kids in an overcrowded building, where there are thirty-five kids or more in a class, Dad feels you're lost in the crowd. The teachers don't even give you enough homework."

"Not enough!" Joey's cry was anguished.

"He thinks you should be in smaller classes with supervised study. He has met the headmaster of a fine small school with an international reputation, and he thinks it would do you a world of good and really help you get into college."

"Is it in Scotland?"

Mrs. Larkin nodded. Joey stopped eating. He thought he was going to be sick.

"It would be a wonderful opportunity," she said thoughtfully.

"Not for me. I'd run away and find a job doing anything before I'd let him send me way off there to school."

"That's wild talk and you know it."

"But it's the way I *feel*. Dad can't stand the idea that one of his sons might not go to college — as if it were an insult to *him!* So he'll try any angle that might get me in."

"Joel, your father is very well known for coming up with the right solution to a problem. He feels that you have a problem and he's found the answer to it. How do you know but what it might be just the right thing for you?"

"It wouldn't, Mum. Besides, Dad has the problem.

129

He's expecting too much of me. It scares me."

"Joel, we both think you can do more than you are doing in school. So far you're not flunking, but you're just sliding through. You never make an extra effort. I'm just as worried as your father is. He didn't want me to mention this to you. But it would be a shock for him to spring it on you suddenly with all his enthusiasm for what he considers a tremendous opportunity."

"Do you want me to go away, too, Mum?"

"Joel, I want what will be best for you, now and in the future. But I'm not sure yet what that is. Perhaps your father has more perspective since he's been away for a while."

"It will wreck my whole Christmas. If I know he's planning to ship me off it will ruin everything, and if I don't know, I'll just worry all the time."

"I shouldn't have told you. But I'm sure Dad will want to talk about it sooner rather than later."

"Probably the minute he's in the door. Joe boy, pack your things! You're off to Scotland. Off with your head!"

Joey made a dramatic gesture that inadvertently shot his plate from the table. It crashed on the floor. At least picking up the pieces gave him something to do. Then he laced on his high boots, found a parka and a ski band for his ears, and opened the back door.

The dry cold air pinched his nose and tingled the top of his head, but the shoveling was hot hard work.

The wind had driven the snow until it was packed almost hard enough for a ski slope.

Joey's path from kitchen door to garage passed the empty cage and reminded him that Bertie must be snowed in somewhere.

When Mrs. Larkin shoved Jock out to help, Joey said, "Answer me a scientific question. If an animal is snowed into a hole, will it smother? Or will it have air enough to keep breathing?"

"If you're talking about Bertie, he can semi-hibernate. Just curl up and sleep and breathe sort of low and not have to eat for three or four days at a time. He's in a better spot than we are. He doesn't have to shovel."

After ten minutes or so Jock jumped over the fresh snow and flung himself down in it, making patterns of footprints and body prints as he leaped and rolled. Joey felt too full of woes to join him. He leaned on his shovel and moped until Mrs. Larkin came out. Thinking to rouse him, she made a snowball and threw it at him unexpectedly.

It didn't hurt, because the snow was so dry the ball fell away into a scattering of flakes. But it was too much for Joey. "You didn't have to throw things at me, too," he muttered.

He trudged off by himself and began digging a useless path from the house across the back lawn to the brook, which ran black and bubbling despite its icy borders. He called, "Bertie!" a few times, but not a chirp sounded in return.

He watched the water a long time, almost hypnotized by its incessant movement. He heard the town plow scraping and banging down the driveway.

He jumped in surprise when close behind him Reino spoke up, "You want to put on some skis or snowshoes and take a hike through the woods? Your ma thought you might like to go looking for coon tracks."

"Oh, I don't know," said Joey dejectedly. "I still have to shovel out by the garage."

"Come walk with me. I'll help you shovel later. We can look for a Christmas tree for the house, too."

"All right." It was a relief to have someone tell him what to do. Retreat to the house on his own after a fuss would have been difficult.

Reino kept snowshoes handy for his wintertime tours of the woods. "I'll take the bear paws. You take the pickerels."

The rounder shape of the bear paws suited Reino's short gait, as he always rolled from side to side when he walked. But even with the long thin pickerel snowshoes, Joey felt awkward. He forgot they wouldn't slide, and then lifted his feet too high and tired quickly. It was a while before an easy rhythm of walking came to him.

Despite the crisp sunlight, it was cold. When he

spoke, he felt as if he were spitting out ice cubes. Reino plodded on. Occasionally he pointed to tracks. "Mice," he announced. Joey laughed at the feathery prints, skittering about.

A rabbit had bounded down the path, in matched hops and unconcern. Then, where the snow was scuffed and stained, the tracks of a fox led to the spot and away. With a worried pang, Joey wondered what would happen if a fox tackled a raccoon? Or a raccoon tackled a fox?

Calling, "Bertie!" Joey detoured around the snow-packed hideaway. "Would I know a coon print if I saw one?" Joey finally asked.

"Sure you would. Just like a thin little hand. Five separate fingerprints and a bit of a palm. You know, either a few foxes sure are busy, or there are a lot more around this year."

"Reino! Remember the frozen fox you brought in four or five years ago?"

"Oh, yes. It died of something right where it was standing in the woods. And it froze that way — head up and tail out and one foot ready to step ahead."

"I wanted to keep it in the freezer, but Mum wouldn't let me. She said it would shock her too much when she opened the chest. But she let me keep it in the garage for a few days. I remember expecting it to thaw out and run off any second. I even took it to school. I carried it in a box and we had to cut a hole in the box for its tail. I can remember Mum running around trying to find a box big enough for a fox and she thought it was so funny when she found one from a fur store. My, that was a long time ago!"

"Long time for you. Short time for me," Reino said thoughtfully. "Each year you ask for a taller Christmas tree."

They found three good ones for Mr. Larkin to choose from, and circled back to the house. With Reino's help, Joey cleared the drifts from the garage doors. They just finished when a taxi hustled down the drive. Mr. Larkin leaped out and Joey momentarily forgot all the feelings that had been seething around in his mind.

There was his father, and he brought with him an electricity of excitement that always struck a reciprocating spark in Joey. In that instant Joey knew he loved his father just as much as he always had, with a real admiring love. And that would make it tougher to go against him. It would be so easy if only he wanted to do what his father wanted him to do.

"Joe!" His father swept him up in a great hug. "Joe! Joe! Joe! I never missed you all as much as this trip. Here's Jerry."

Joey automatically stuck out his arms and Mr. Larkin piled things into them. Boxes and books and traveling bags. In the excitement of seeing his father, Joey only gave Jerry a quick look. But even that was enough to see that he looked thinner and had big circles under his eyes.

The next few hours were full of happy confusion. Wherever he went, Joey seemed to hear his father's voice rising and falling, talk flowing as incessantly as waves on a beach. The whole house felt different, as if it were a shell no longer abandoned, but once again housing the creature who gave it life.

Everyone talked of plans to do this or that and when to do it, and Mr. Larkin listed the important things on his mind, while Mrs. Larkin just sat and laughed. "I can't keep up with it all. Just tell me what you want and when — but don't ask me to be organized."

"Tomorrow morning at nine we will all go to the woods and fetch home the Christmas tree," Mr. Larkin decided. "Then we'll go to church."

"Then we'll eat," said Joey.

"Tomorrow afternoon we can see the outdoor Christmas pageant over in Bayport," Mrs. Larkin hoped.

Joey had keyed himself up to expect a talk with his father almost at once. But with all these activities perhaps it would be after Christmas before his father considered Joey and his problems. With excitement and holiday gaiety taking over, Joey decided he didn't want to face his problems himself until after Christmas. But if he had a chance, he wanted to talk to Jerry before his father cornered him.

That evening he helped his mother clear away the dinner dishes and straighten up the kitchen, listening all the time for a scratch or a bang at the door.

"You'd think old Bertie would have woken up and dug himself out by now! Do you think he's all right? Or he's starved and frozen somewhere?"

"I remember a raccoon coat I had years ago," Mrs. Larkin began.

"Oh, Mum! Please!"

"Don't worry, Joel. I didn't mean that Bertie might be trapped somewhere. I meant a raccoon's fur is so warm. He couldn't freeze. He isn't meant to be an indoor animal. You forget that when you think of him as your pet."

"I suppose so." Joey fetched a pack of cards to play solitaire on the kitchen table. He intended to spend the evening where he could hear if Bertie came to the door. But Mr. Larkin objected. "You must come to the Music Room. I've told Jerry we certainly expect a concert from him."

"I'm waiting to see if Bertie shows up for his supper. He lives outside somewhere now — and we haven't seen him since the storm." Joey looked at the kitchen clock. "Dad, if he doesn't come in twenty minutes, I'll be down."

"Can't you leave some food on the doorstep for him?"

"It would freeze. I'll be down — in twenty minutes." Joey made his voice sound much firmer than he felt. Perhaps if his father allowed him one small concession like this, he'd listen and understand when the large problem arose.

"Well, all right, animal lover. Bring down some Cokes for all of us when you come."

The twenty minutes passed with no sign of Bertie. Joey stood outside and called. The vast dark, the stabbing cold and the whiplash wind made it a cruel night. Joey shivered. He left a hopeful offering of raisins on the doorstep. His mother came in to fetch a plate of cookies and saw him scattering the raisins.

"Placating the gods?"

Joey shrugged. "Maybe I am."

The next morning the raisins had disappeared, but Joey was not jubilant. There wasn't a single paw print near the door that looked raccoonish. In fact, the only prints were Lancelot's and he wagged his tail contentedly and took one more swipe over the doorstep with his tongue. "Pig!" Joey said to Lancelot.

After breakfast they strapped on skis and snow shoes. Joey led them to each of the trees Reino suggested. Mr. Larkin chose the tallest. He could have chopped it down in six or seven good whacks, but he carried out the family tradition of handing the ax to each one in turn while they sang "O Tannenbaum."

Until now Joey always enjoyed finding the tree and chopping at it and singing. But this year he felt outside it all, as if he were a stranger observing his family. Surely *they* were the different ones — not he. He was glad only the trees and the birds were watching them.

The tree fell with a sighing of branches and splash of snow. Joey helped lash it to the toboggan, and then snowshoed ahead, pulling the tree. The tune "O Tannenbaum" stuck annoyingly in his head and he tried whistling it to get rid of it. By the time they reached the house it had even cheered him up, and he wondered if perhaps there weren't quite a few other families who chopped their own trees and maybe even sang "O Tannenbaum."

Jock wanted to trim the tree as soon as they reached the house.

"Tonight," said Mr. Larkin. "You can't rush trimming a tree. I'm a sentimentalist. I want a leisurely evening of tree-trimming with my favorite Christmas carols playing on the victrola."

"Victrola!" Jerry groaned. "Dad, you really are pretending to be an old, old patriarch!"

Mrs. Larkin sighed. "Whatever happened to lovely sounding words like victrola and veranda and vestibule — "

"They are just retired," said Mr. Larkin. "Memories — like the things they were named for. But we have nice-sounding new words like geodesic and polyethylene."

"Church is still a good word," Mrs. Larkin said, "and if we don't hurry, we'll be late."

It seemed to Joey that they hurried all day, except when they stood stamping their icy feet, waiting on the main street of a neighboring seacost town to see an outdoor Nativity pageant.

Joey was impatient. He really wanted to stay home and listen for Bertie, hoping that when darkness came, the raccoon would wake up and end his two-day fast with a trip to the house. But Joey did realize that even though he felt impatient with family projects and inclined to go off on his own, Christmas was absolutely the wrong time to protest. Even though the pageant was beautiful and convincing, he was glad when it was over.

As the car stopped so the garage door could open on its electronic beam control, Joey suddenly saw a dark shadow bounding over the snow. He yelled, "Bertie!"

The shadow stood motionless, then slowly the head turned. Two red eyes gleamed out toward them and then too many voices from the car joined in, calling, "Bertie!" The raccoon whisked away.

"At least I know he's alive," Joey said happily.

"How do you know it was Bertie?" Jock asked. "There's lots of other raccoons around."

"Jock!" Mrs. Larkin whispered. "Where's your Christmas spirit?"

Joey swung the flashlight beam over the snow.

"See? He's been running around and around the house, trying to get in. No other raccoon would do that, Jock. I knew I should have stayed home to take care of him. Maybe he's waiting at the back door." Joey ran around the house, and was terribly disappointed not to see Bertie's bulky shadow on the doorstep or in the yard. "Bertie? Oh, Bertie!"

Jerry unlocked the back door and stuck his head out. "Any luck?"

"No. I just hope he's hungry enough to come back."

Joey ate his supper alone in the kitchen, while the others snacked in the dining room. Bertie did not return. But when they trimmed the tree in the living room, Joey joined them because it sounded as if they were having too good a time to miss.

Jock supervised the assembling of the six strings of colored lights, and Mrs. Larkin their artistic placement. After that everyone sorted through the huge box of ornaments, looking for favorite decorations. Joey liked to make things, and up until now had been proud of his achievements — the silvered and gilded pine cones, the wobbly Santa Claus of cloth with a glued-on cotton-wool beard, the angel with a yo-yo head and cardboard wings, and the tin can tops cut into star shapes and splashed with sequins. But suddenly they all looked handmade and he hated them. He quietly picked out all his handiwork and found a paper

140

bag to hide it in behind the couch before his mother could hang any up with some embarrassingly loving remark.

When the tree was well-laden with gay and gaudy balls and bells, shining icicles and fluorescent stars, the annual tinsel disagreement arose.

"Give me a couple of handfuls and I'll stand back and heave it," said Joey.

"It always looks terrible when you do it that way," Jock complained. "It has to go on piece by piece."

Joey, impatient to see the final result, threw a handful at the tree. Most of it slid to the floor, but some dangled crookedly from the branches.

"Don't!" said Jock. "You'll spoil it."

"Oh, all right." Joey handed over the tinsel packages. "I'll come back in an hour and you'll only be halfway around the tree, fuss-pot."

Then four cars drove in and some of Jerry's friends and Mr. and Mrs. Larkin's friends arrived all at once. The whole house was soon full of lights, music and chatter.

Around midnight Mr. and Mrs. Larkin went to bed. Joey started to go to bed, too, but then he decided he wanted very much to talk to Jerry before his father caught up with him, and see what his brother thought about Dad's wanting to send him away to school. It might be a good idea to have more practice at discussing the subject before Dad started on it. So he sat on the living room couch, waiting for Jerry's friends to leave.

He looked at a skiing magazine for a while and then turned off all but the tree lights, enjoying the tricks the colors played on familiar objects in the room. But suddenly the colors blurred into rainbows as his eyelids fell. Sleep heavily overcame him.

A great crash woke Joey with a heart-thumping jolt. He tried to sit up, but something sharp jabbed at his face. The large crashing sound died away into more fragile tinklings and pops, as if thousands of pieces of glass were shattering one after the other. As his eyes widened, he saw a scramble of colored lights on the floor. And through it all rose Bertie's whirring cry, in panic.

"Help!" yelled Joey, as he pushed the tip of the Christmas tree out of his eye and tried to spring up. "Somebody! Come quick!"

6

MR. LARKIN snapped on the overhead light as Joey tried to get at the wall plug by the couch and pull out the tree lights.

"Watch it!" Mr. Larkin warned. "That looks like wall-to-wall broken glass under foot."

"But Bertie's caught under the tree. Help me get it off him."

Picking up the tree proved an ornery job. Branches prickled, and he had to reach gingerly past broken pieces of glass to get a good grip on the trunk. But finally his father pulled the tree up, while Mrs. Larkin stood by to straighten the stand and Joey to rescue Bertie.

Once the branches were clear, Bertie still lay on the floor squealing and Joey dropped to his knees and slowly put out his hand. Bertie immediately chewed at Joey's knuckles.

"He's not biting hard, so he's not mad. But I guess he's too frightened to move, unless his back is broken."

"If he survived falling out of a tree, he'll survive having a tree fall on him," Mr. Larkin said in a disgusted voice. "What a mess."

"What is Bertie doing in the house anyway, Joel?" asked Mrs. Larkin. "You know better than to bring him in if you aren't watching him every minute."

"I fell asleep on the couch and I don't know how he sneaked in. What time is it?"

Mr. Larkin looked at his watch. "Quarter past one in the morning. There goes that night's sleep."

"I'm sorry, Dad."

Jerry appeared, still dressed but looking sleepy. "Did you know the kitchen door was blown open and it's freezing in there?"

"Bertie! Did you open the storm door and the kitchen door all by yourself?" Joey asked. Bertie decided it was safe to move after all and he rolled over, still chewing at Joey's hand and pushing it with all four feet. His bright eyes gleamed up happily at Joey.

As they all stared down at him, he stopped chewing long enough to do what Joey insisted was smiling, or the equivalent of it. He pulled his lips back, and with his mouth open, made breathy little noises — soft half-grunts, half-squeaks that seemed to have a relaxed and tender meaning. Joey leaned over him and rubbed his head on Bertie's soft stomach. Bertie clutched Joey's ears and kept on smiling.

"Oh, Joel — do watch out for your eyes!" groaned Mrs. Larkin.

"He's not going to hurt me, Mum. He's playing." Joey's face turned red, as he almost stood on his head. "He's being awfully gentle."

"I think he knows he's been naughty and he's purposely trying to bewitch us," said Mrs. Larkin.

"Well, I'm not bewitched," said Mr. Larkin. "Did anyone lock the kitchen door tonight?"

They all shook their heads. "Lancelot wanted out about midnight," Jerry said. "I let him out in a hurry and may not have shut either the storm door or the inside door tight. Bertie may just have wiggled the latch on the outside door and then leaned on the kitchen door, and in he flew — "

"He has a lot of weight to lean with now, doesn't he!" Mr. Larkin studied the animal. "He's tremendous."

"He weighs about sixteen pounds," said Joey. "It's hard to tell because he lops over the edge of the bathroom scales and his tail always hangs off."

"I don't dare argue with him any more," said Mrs. Larkin. "Joel, you must put him out now. We all need our sleep."

"All right. But I'll feed him first."

Putting him out was easier intended than done. Bertie had slept well during his absence and the warmth of the house brought out his liveliness. He was wide awake and ready for a grand playtime. He couldn't understand why Joey sat yawning at the table instead of rolling about on the floor with him. He dashed around, pretending to attack Joey's feet. He stood up and tried to search Joey's pants' pockets.

"Look, Bertie — " Joey said. "I'm thrilled you're back, see? You're my absolutely favorite animal. You're my buddy. I love you. But I don't like to play at two o'clock in the morning."

Bertie rolled over and smiled up at him, looking as lovable as a stuffed Teddy bear. He made his funny little happy sounds.

"Oh, aha-aha-aha yourself!" Joey breathed back. Then he scooped Bertie from the floor and hugged him. He stood rocking the raccoon in his arms, his head down against Bertie's warm bushy back. "Merry Christmas, old Bertie. You're the best present I ever had from anybody all my life."

146

Bertie disliked any tight grasp and struggled to free himself. "So I hate to put you outdoors," Joey finished, "but I have to."

Bertie was slipping down his trouser leg as Joey pulled the door open and dumped the coon on the step. Before he could shut the door, Bertie backed through the gap in a flash and galloped across the kitchen floor. His rear end was so heavy and his tail so emphatic that this bumbling gallop usually made Joey laugh.

"Oh, come on, Bertie. Be a help," Joey begged. "I'm tired."

It took three more minutes of dodging and chasing before Joey finally caught him. He yelled for Jerry to open the door and together they managed it.

They checked and locked the doors and turned off the lights as quickly as they could. But they could hear Bertie running around the house, making loud screeches of protest and banging at the doors for some time.

Joey trailed Jerry down to the Music Room. "Are you awake enough to talk?"

"Not really. That is, if you want any sense from me. I've never been so tired in all my life."

"Then get into bed while I talk to you," said Joey, sitting down on the piano bench. "I want to ask you some questions."

"Uhhh," yawned Jerry. He stripped off his sweater and shirt and trousers, socks and shoes, left them in a heap on the floor and lay down on the couch behind the piano. He pulled blankets up to his chin and shut his eyes. It wasn't like Jerry to be so abrupt, even with his brothers.

"I know it's late," Joey apologized.

"Late!" Jerry didn't even open his eyes. "This is early. It's the earliest I've hit the sack since Thanksgiving."

"You mean you sit around and talk this late every night?"

"No. I study. Sometimes until four in the morning. And I start practicing again at eight."

"You have homework in classes? Besides just playing the piano?"

"Um. I have very complex homework in Harmony and Music Theory. I have to read tons of stuff on Music History and write papers. And other courses, too. Just the class work and homework alone would fill up a year at college. But the piano's like a monster. The more you work at it, the more demanding it gets."

"I thought you loved playing so much that you never minded how much time you spent at it. And if you were so good at it, why do you have to practice all that much?"

"I did love playing. All the time. But I was playing for myself. Maybe to convince myself that I was pretty great and I had my future all cut out for me." Jerry suddenly sat up and opened his eyes. Joey was surprised to see he was pale and sweating. "You know something, Joey — I'm not pretty great. I'm pretty awful."

"You couldn't be! You always sound great to me."

"Are you a piano teacher? And I don't mean like Miss Mixter. Sure — she's good as a teacher for around here out in the country. And she got me started. But am I ever far behind! There are kids in my class who have already been studying with top-notch teachers since they were nine years old. Or going to professional high schools with high standards in some of the big cities, so they've had more of a music background than I do. I'm beginning to wonder how they ever let me into the Conservatory anyway."

"You still sound good to me," Joey insisted.

"And what are you?" Jerry pointed an accusing finger at Joey. "Are you a concert pianist? Are you a professor of music at the Conservatory? No. You're an untrained relative. With an untrained ear. There are one hundred and thirty-five kids in a class of one hundred and thirty-six that are better pianists than I am." He lay down again, with the sigh of a deflating balloon.

"You've only been there three and a half months."

"That's long enough," Jerry whispered. "Long enough to find out I'm no good. And I haven't got guts enough to quit."

"You mean — you don't want to go back?"

"No. I don't. But I will."

"Sure you will, Jerry. You've just got too tired and discouraged. It will all be better after vacation. You'll go back and stun them all."

"I'll go back and I'll struggle on — but I'll only be kidding myself. And Dad. You see, Joey — I could admit to myself that I'd made a mistake. But not to Dad. Did you hear him talking to Mr. Butler tonight? Dad was calling me the next Horowitz and talking about how marvelous it was in a plain practical family like the Larkins to have a real artist at last. His son. He'd sired a concert pianist."

Jerry's words reminded Joey that it was his own problem with Dad that he'd wanted to discuss. But it just didn't seem the right time. It was Jerry who needed comforting.

"I still say you'll be all right when you go back after a vacation. Maybe the first few months are like stage fright and when you relax it will be better."

"I wish I thought so." Jerry closed his eyes again. "I wish I weren't scared to death."

"Scared of what?"

"Of all the things I thought I could do. And I can't." He shivered.

His words were spoken in such a desperate tone that Joey felt uncomfortable. There didn't seem to be any real way in which he could help, so he picked up Jerry's clothes and folded them and put another blanket over Jerry. "You want the light out?"

"Please. And don't go blabbing to Mum what I said. I'm going back for Dad's sake, but they'll fire me out by spring vacation. I just hope Dad'll be in Afghanistan when it happens."

"If I know you, it won't happen," Joey said firmly.

"If I know me. That's the problem. I didn't know me at all."

Joey sat on the bench, waiting to see if Jerry said any more. When he didn't and he seemed to have stopped shivering and fallen asleep, Joey turned out the lights and walked quietly through the house. He sat in the dark on his bed, staring out at the dull night for a long time, his thoughts and ideas confused and troubled. If Jerry, confident, capable Jerry, decided he didn't know himself, how was unconfident Joey ever going to discover himself?

It was his mother who was troubled next morning, however, as she surveyed the damaged tree. "Some of those ornaments have been around for years," she sighed. "This is one Christmas we'll never forget."

Jock spoke up. "The Chinese have the Year of the Dragon and the Year of the Monkey. You ought to call this the Year of the Raccoon."

"Each one of those animals stands for something — the kind of year it's supposed to be," Mrs. Larkin remembered. "I wonder what the raccoon stands for."

"It looks like a year of havoc and destruction," said Mr. Larkin.

"No, it isn't!" Joey protested. "Not the whole year anyway. I mean, he's done one or two bad things. But look at all the good things he's done."

"Name three good things," said Jock. "Go ahead. Name three."

Joey hesitated. His love for Bertie and his pride in having him for a pet were good things to him, but perhaps he was the only one who saw them that way after all.

"I can think of three bad things," Jock said quickly. "Jerry's finger. My fish. And the Christmas tree. The Year of the Raccoon is a bad year."

What if it was? Joey's worries spurted up in his mind. What if this was the year his father finally realized Joey was a pretty poor sample of Larkins? What if his parents decided Bertie was too destructive and banished him? What if this was the year he was banished, too — to a school in Scotland?

Joey's stricken look reached Mrs. Larkin. "That's just your view, Jock. You can think of good things about the year of the raccoon, can't you, Joel? I can."

"Sure, but it's hard to explain so it sounds to you as good as it does to me. I mean — I have a lot of fun with Bertie. And I've learned a lot from him. And I

like him much more than poor old Lancelot. I mean —
who else around here has a raccoon?"

"Lots of lucky people don't," said Jock. "Mum,
are we going to save this tree, or find another one?"

"It's easier to fix another one," Mr. Larkin decided.
"It would take a week and a box of Bandaids to untan-
gle all those broken ornaments. Who wants to come?"

But everyone except Joey had plans. Joey laced
his boots on and followed just far enough behind so
that Mr. Larkin wouldn't consider it a good time for
a discussion of his future. When the path was wide
enough for them to snowshoe side by side, Joey
quickly asked his father questions about the trees and
the map they once talked of making of the plantings.

"Sure I want one. It would be great fun to do. But
I never seem to have the time."

Mr. Larkin whacked this tree down without ceremony and no one sang over it. When they brought it
back to the house, Jerry was backing the station
wagon out of the garage to take Mrs. Larkin on a last-
minute shopping trip. "We're going to buy some ornaments and tree lights. Any shopping you want to do,
Joey?"

Joey suddenly felt numb. He'd bought a head of
Beethoven for Jerry at a church fair sale last summer,
when it seemed like the absolutely perfect gift. He
even gift-wrapped it last August. And he'd bought
some lipstick for his mother, because she sometimes

forgot to put it on mornings when his father wasn't around, and he didn't think she looked right without it. He had a model of a dinosaur for Jock to make. And a book about modern Finland for Reino. But he hadn't decided what to buy for his father. Here it was the day before Christmas and he didn't have a thing for him!

"What's the matter, Joel?" asked his mother. "You look funny."

"I'd better come," he said.

"Get your mother to do your errands," Mr. Larkin called impatiently. "I'm going to need help switching these trees."

"Never mind," said Joey desperately. "I don't know what I want anyway. Maybe I could catch a bus and go in this afternoon."

"Wait a minute, Ruth!" Mr. Larkin said expansively. "Never mind looking for ornaments. We'll make our own. This will be a real old-fashioned Christmas tree. We'll spend Christmas Eve by the fireside — popping corn and stringing it, and stringing cranberries. And whatever else you put on an old-fashioned tree. Cornucopias! Get what we need, dear, and we'll have a wonderful evening doing it."

"But we spent last evening decorating a tree!" Jock objected.

"It might be easier to find ornaments than popcorn and cranberries," Mrs. Larkin said softly.

"Never!" Mr. Larkin was firm.

"Oh, dear!" she groaned. "I thought this would be a serene Christmas because everything was done ahead of time." They drove off.

"There should be a scientific way to do this efficiently," Mr. Larkin announced as he surveyed the catastrophe inside. But there wasn't. Pulling the lights and few unbroken ornaments from the tree and sweeping up the debris took an hour. "For once I wish I was in Burma or wherever I could clap my hands and tell the houseboys to clean it up."

Joey worked as fast as he could. Christmas without a present for his father was unthinkable, and he had to get into town somehow. He was worrying so hard about what he could find for his father that he didn't really listen to what Mr. Larkin was saying. He just grunted when some kind of response seemed needed.

Finally Mr. Larkin stopped sweeping and stared at Joey. "Look, this is a great opportunity. Can't you show a little enthusiasm for the chance of a lifetime?"

Joey's heart thudded. His father must have been telling him about the school in Scotland. What could he say? "I won't go!" or "I don't want to go!" Or fall on his knees and say, "Please don't send me away!"

If Mr. Larkin had been carrying a brief case or holding a slide rule, Joey would have been too awed to challenge him. But his father looked so out of place, standing there with a broom and dust pan in his hand, that it gave Joey courage.

First he asked cautiously to make sure, "Just where did you say this place is?"

"About fifty miles north of Edinburgh. On the sea. Beautiful country. You'll love it. Boys from all over the world. Fascinating chaps. Headmaster believes in discipline plus development. It's not all studies — there's athletics, too. Soccer. Ability and agility is one of their mottoes. All that."

"Cold showers, short pants and knee socks?" asked Joey flatly, dredging out of his stunned mind a newsphoto of Prince Charles at his rugged school.

"Those are minor matters. No different from wearing cold chinos and wet torn sneakers all winter at a New England prep school. It's the inner man that counts."

"When did you want to send me away?"

"The logical time would be next fall. I could even take you along wherever I go next summer. It may be Iran. And send you to Scotland from there. But the way things stand now, maybe we should fly you over for next term. Along with Christmas tidings, the mail today brought two warning notices."

"In what?" Joey sparred for time. He knew only too well. They were flunk warnings in math and French. He felt as if math were a jig-saw puzzle, because everyone told him it all made sense when the pieces were fitted together properly. "It all adds up," or "It all balances out." Or "If you'd just do it right, you'd see." But he was convinced there were pieces purposely missing from his set of jig-saw puzzles, always. Unless maybe it was his brain that missed and skipped and didn't understand. That could be. He gave a long sigh.

And French. He dreaded the teacher to the point where he felt sick when he went into her classroom. He would sit there and first his stomach would lurch and then his hands would freeze and then his mind would close. He was helpless.

"I'd still have to take math and French over there, wouldn't I?" Joey asked.

"And Latin. They have Greek, but it's not required. And sciences. English history, and American history from a British point of view. That should be interesting."

"I think it would be a great school for Jock," Joey said slowly. "And I think it would kill me."

There was a deep silence, while Mr. Larkin looked at Joey in complete surprise.

Then Joey went on. "I could take the discipline and the cold showers, too. And I'd probably like soccer. But I'd never be any good at the studies. I'd just be an international failure. And then where would you be?"

"What do you mean? Where would I be? It's you. Where will you be?"

157

"No, I meant you. You'd have a son who couldn't do what you want him to do. You're used to telling people in factories what to do. Then they make a superhuman effort and do it for you somehow. But I'm not a factory or a product. I'm just a personal bottleneck."

Now he'd said what he honestly felt, Joey's breathing calmed down and his heart stopped pounding. But he couldn't move until he heard his father's verdict. That's what he was sure it would be — a judgment — a sentence.

Mr. Larkin swept at a speck on the rug and kept sweeping at it. "Look, Joe — life wouldn't be worth a hoot without problems, and I'm extremely fond of you, you old personal bottleneck. Possibly, just possibly, the solution I see as best for your problem might not be the easiest solution for you to handle alone. But have you any other ideas to offer?"

"Remember when we were eating clams last summer? You said any time I failed or dropped a subject I closed another door on some opportunity? I worry about the doors slamming, you know. Especially when I don't have any idea what I want to do. But maybe I haven't been trying as hard as I could. Maybe if I spend more time studying and try harder — "

Mr. Larkin pounded with the broom. "I've heard that from you before. Oh, how I've heard that from you. But I'll make a deal with you. I won't decide right this minute. I'll wait until your mid-year marks are in. If you don't flunk the two courses you have warnings in, you can stay here through this June. I'll wait until then to decide what to do with you. How's that?"

Joey looked at his father. He didn't like his saying, "I'll decide what to do with you." He wanted to be able to decide what to do with himself.

But at least it was a postponement of doom, and in some ways it was more than he hoped for.

"All right. I'll make my New Year's resolutions early. On Christmas Eve."

"Good." His father put down the broom at last, as if it were a threat no longer needed. "Now, let's stand up the new tree. It's a better shape, but it sure is bare. Joey, how about pine cones to hang on it? Could you rush out and find some?"

It was the last thing Joey wanted to do. The early snow covered everything — fallen cones, the green ground pine and partridge berries his mother had wanted for table decorations. He'd have to hack cones from any branches he could reach.

"Where are the trees that have the best cones?" he asked. It would be handy to have that map his father wanted.

That was it — something his father wanted. Something he needed! He wouldn't have to go shopping for a present after all. He could make one. Now he

159

was glad of an excuse to run to the woods. "I'll find the pine cones," he promised.

Joey put on snowshoes and took a clipboard and paper. Not far beyond the pond, he found Reino stacking wood. When he explained his project, Reino said, "I'll come with you. Maybe I can help."

Even with the snowshoes, it took them two hours to walk around, making notes and picking out landmarks.

When they returned to the house, Joey found the large aerial photographs of the woods and some geodetic survey maps of the area his father had bought. Joey made a rough sketch on old wrapping paper and Reino checked him out on where the stands of fir, spruce, hemlock, red pine, white pine, balsam, cedar and Norway pine were, and the few Finnish pines that were Reino's proud project.

"I don't mind walking over it all, but I'd never have the patience to draw it," Reino said with admiration. "Hope you get it done before tomorrow. Guess I'll go along now, Joey. Merry Christmas."

"See you tomorrow. You'll be coming to Christmas dinner, won't you?"

"Your ma asked me. She always does. But I don't know, Joe. I'm kind of tired. I might just sleep all day tomorrow."

Joey suddenly wondered what was bothering Reino. He was usually such an up-early, don't-waste-a-minute Finn.

"You have to come! It wouldn't be Christmas dinner without you. Did you know, when I was little and Mum told me you came from way up in Finland above the Arctic Circle where there were lots of reindeer, I always wanted to ask you if you'd ever met Santa Claus? Until I was six, anyway."

Reino laughed. "Well, maybe I'll come. It wouldn't be Christmas without being with you, Joe."

"Jerry and I'll pick you up at twelve-thirty," Joey promised. "Now — I've got to find a whopping piece of cardboard for this map."

Joey searched closets and cupboards, but nothing was big or clean enough. In desperation he went to his mother. "Can you take me into town? I'm making Dad a present, but I need some cardboard and ink and paints."

"Oh, dear! I was just going to start dinner — the special scalloped oysters Dad always wants on Christmas Eve. Is it vital?"

"It's desperate."

"I guess we can make it before the stores close. We'll just have a late dinner."

When they returned, Joey started to carry his things into the Music Room to work on a large table there. But he found Jerry and four of his friends with a record player resounding loudly. To his surprise, it was jazz, a sudden change from Jerry's usual classics.

His mother dashed about distractedly in the kitchen,

and the table there was piled with boxes of uncooked whole cranberries and unpopped corn that had taken her so long to find earlier in the day.

His father sat in the library, impatiently awaiting his old-fashioned tree-trimming party. The dining room table was all set for supper. Joey retreated to work on the floor of his bedroom. He enjoyed making school maps with lots of colors and careful ink lines and lettering, so he quickly became absorbed in his work. Mrs. Larkin called him twice to come to supper.

As soon as they pushed back from the table, Mr. Larkin said, "Now — we'll all go in the living room and pop the corn and string the cranberries and sing Christmas carols."

"Just give me time to clean up the kitchen, dear," Mrs. Larkin suggested.

"I'll help," said Jerry. "There doesn't seem to be anything else to do."

"Then I'll work on my combustion engine till you're ready," Jock announced. "I want to finish it in case good old Santa read the science catalogs I left on Mum's bureau, and brings me some new models."

"Joey, you and I will start the fire and gild a few pine cones for the tree."

"I'm sorry. I haven't finished a present I'm making. I'll be there as soon as I can."

"Last minute Larkin again, eh? And poor Father

is left all alone on Christmas Eve." He gave a mock gulp of sorrow. But everyone rushed to finish his tasks, except Joey. If he rushed, he'd smudge something. Dimly he heard their voices, and once in a while he heard the lid of the corn popper bang and then the scatter-rattle of the hard corn thrown against the wire mesh.

There was a knock at his door. "Don't come in!" he yelled.

"It's me, dear," said his mother. "We don't know what to do about Bertie. He's crashing against the back door and screeching. He sounds so cross we don't dare take care of him."

"Murgatroyd!" muttered Joey. "Why does he have to be a creature of habit. Right now." He stuck his head into the living room. So far only a few strings of cranberries adorned the tree. "Those berries don't look very red."

"They should," Jerry told him. "Everyone I've strung is covered with blood from my pricked fingers."

"Guess you're not very red-blooded!" joked Joey.

"Jerry!" exclaimed Mrs. Larkin. "Maybe that's why you look so pale. You're anemic! You should go see Dr. Harvey during vacation."

"Oh, Mum! I'm not anemic." Jerry sounded disgusted.

"Great guns, Ruth," exploded Mr. Larkin. "The

163

boy's just tired. He's been working hard."

"But I don't like the way he looks." Mrs. Larkin defended her motherly instincts.

"It's just city pallor," Jerry said quickly.

"All he needs is a good vacation," declared Mr. Larkin. "Go feed your beast, Joey, so you can join us."

Joey placed a chair against the door from the kitchen to the hall, so no one could walk in unexpectedly and let Bertie escape to the rest of the house. Then he opened the back door and Bertie burst in, bristling. He looked puffed with indignation at waiting in the cold and he kept trying to climb up the cupboard doors to the counter while Joey assembled his food.

"Mind your manners," Joey said in the firm tone that used to slow Bertie down. Placing the dish on the floor, he just pulled his fingers out of the way as Bertie dove into it so fiercely that raisins and crackers flew out in all directions. Bertie tramped all over them with a determination that sobered Joey. He opened the refrigerator door to take out a bottle of milk, and Bertie's head, shoulders and front paws were suddenly in the way so he couldn't close the door. Bertie caught hold of a pound of hamburg and thumped down on the floor.

Joey reached for it. Bertie cradled it, squashing the meat against his chest and screeching.

"Don't stand there saying 'It's mine. It's mine,'"

Joey said. "Give it to me. It's Mother's. She'll clunk me if you eat it."

But Bertie did not respond to Joey's conversational tone, either. He turned his back, unwrapped the meat and began stuffing himself. For the first time Joey didn't dare take something away from him.

"I've created a monster," he moaned. All he could do was stand there until Bertie ate almost the whole pound of hamburg. The last little pieces he rolled around in his busy black paws as if he were shaping a little bun to fry.

Joey couldn't help laughing. "All you need is an apron, you nut!"

Bertie dropped the little wad of meat, sat down glassy-eyed, his stomach ballooning furrily. He belched. He looked surprised, and then he belched again.

"At least you're too stuffed to play for hours. Out you go!" Joey grabbed Bertie and set him down in the snow outside before he could react. Joey jumped inside and locked the door. When he peeked out a window, he saw Bertie shake himself with one more violent burp and then lumber like a stuffed bear around the corner of the house.

"Maybe he'll go hibernate," Joey said, surprised to find he really wished it. "For over Christmas, anyway."

He unbarricaded the kitchen and dashed back to his map. In another half hour he finished it and spread it carefully to dry. He could wrap it first thing in the morning.

Then he joined the tree-trimmers, who all seemed to be yawning.

"Of course in the old days," Mr. Larkin was saying, "they used real candles on the trees."

"I think we've had enough disasters without that," Mrs. Larkin said flatly.

"We have certainly festooned the tree. Joey, how do you like it?" Mr. Larkin asked.

"It's fine, I guess. It — doesn't shine very much, does it? Glitter and tinsel and lights make a lot of difference, don't they?"

"That's what we've become used to," Mr. Larkin said sadly. "A tinsel world. That's all. A tinsel world."

"I'm going to do something I haven't done since you were little," Mrs. Larkin decided. "I'm going to read to you."

Joey sat on the floor by the fire. His mother read the story of the Nativity in the musically familiar words of the Bible. Beyond the windows the sky was the dark deep blue of the Christmas cards that always showed wise men and camels. The thought that it was the same sky above and the same planet still spinning about in the universe that had spun beneath Bethlehem so long ago came through Joey's mind with a shock. Time

meant nothing for a few seconds, and the world became an awesome wonder. Joey felt the way he did
outdoors on a crisp winter night, looking up into galaxies and galaxies of stars stretching out to infinity, and
wanting to understand it all, and finding it far beyond
understanding.

Then Mrs. Larkin picked up *Wind in the Willows*
and read the Dulce Domum chapter about the field
mice coming to sing carols to Rat and Mole. The feeling of universes faded away and the coziness of the
room crept around them. The sharp green smell of
the freshly cut tree appropriately spiced the story of
the woods animals on Christmas Eve.

Mrs. Larkin read the last sentence, which was about
Mole tucked into his own bed. *"But it was good to
think he had this to come back to, this place which was
all his own, these things which were so glad to see him
again and could always be counted upon for the same
simple welcome."*

"I wonder if that's the way Bertie feels about our
house," said Joey. "Or does he think his hole outdoors
is home? It must be hard to figure out two completely
different worlds like that — when you've only got a
raccoon brain to work with."

"Don't scorn a raccoon brain," Mr. Larkin told him.
"When Bertie figures out that he likes our world best,
we are going to have one large hairy problem."

Joey, thinking of Bertie and his determined eating of

the pound of hamburg, kept silent. He didn't want to disturb the peace of Christmas Eve.

"Look at the time!" Mrs. Larkin was surprised. "Midnight. Merry Christmas everyone!"

"It's too bad Bertie isn't in the house," said Jock to everyone's amazement.

"Why? You never want him around."

"Because at midnight all the animals are supposed to be able to talk — to tell what they were doing when Christ was born and how they took care of him and what they brought for presents. I'd just like to hear what the raccoons did! Probably brought a nice fresh fish."

Joey's eyes flashed.

"Peace, peace, and to bed," ordered Mrs. Larkin. "Tomorrow is another day. Or rather, today is."

But before the Larkins yawned off to bed, they carried in their presents and placed them under the tree. "Just one final goodnight thought," Mr. Larkin suggested. "We will inspect every door and make sure that our tree-climbing friend can't possibly get in anywhere tonight."

"Wouldn't he have a ball opening all those packages!" laughed Joey. "But first he'd eat up the tree — all those strings of cranberries and popcorn. I can just see him slurping them down like strings of spaghetti!"

Whether it was worrying about Bertie spending a gay night unwrapping boxes or worrying about Bertie changing from baby pet to grown-up creature, Joey spent a restless night.

For the first time he didn't mind their not hanging Christmas stockings any more and rushing out of bed at daybreak to pillage them.

Then Jock stuck his head in and yelled, "We can't open presents till we've had breakfast, and everyone's ready but you."

Joey remembered the map and hastily pulled on his clothes. "Is there just one big piece of wrapping paper left anywhere I could have?" Joey asked his mother as she poured his orange juice.

"I'm afraid not."

"There's never anything left for me — ever," Joey said in disgust. "I suppose I'll have to tie this up with my own shoe laces, too. It's my present for Dad."

"I'll find you something. Turn the eggs."

She came back with some shelf paper and bright yarn. With relief, Joey slipped the long roll behind the tree, just before Mr. Larkin walked into the living room, rubbing his hands.

Mrs. Larkin put Christmas music on the hi-fi, and they sat around opening packages.

Mr. Larkin had bought his presents in Scotland, everything from sweaters and bright knit tams to bagpipes, which delighted Jerry. "They may not let me back in the Conservatory with these, but I can certainly express my frustrations with them."

169

When they were almost through, Joey realized the present for his father had been shoved out of sight. He found it behind the couch and handed it to him. "Santa Claus almost didn't get here with this."

Mr. Larkin shook the neat roll of paper and rattled it in the time-honored tradition of guessing. "I just can't imagine. A fishing rod for a dwarf?"

Joey grinned.

"A collapsible dust-mop handle? A thin thin super-light telescope? An ultra-long kaleidoscope?"

"An expandable knot hole?" suggested Jerry.

"A petrified laser-ray?" asked Jock.

"Old bull fight posters, maybe?" Mr. Larkin slowly untied the yarn bow. He enjoyed making a production out of package opening. He unrolled the map with the flourish of a herald and a proclamation.

"Say, now! This is really something." Mr. Larkin hastily cleared a space on the floor and smoothed out the map. "*A map of the Tree Farm of Rory Larkin — at Christmas, 1965. By the U.S. Geodetic Survey, Reino Maki and Joe Larkin.* So this is what kept you busy while we popped the corn! It's just great!"

The family crowded around. "It looks like a professional piece of work," Mrs. Larkin said proudly.

"It's a usable and important document," said Mr. Larkin. "Ruth, first thing tomorrow we'll take this into town and have it framed. And we'll hang it in the library."

"What's this fancy X here, Joey?" Jerry asked. "Or rather, it's an X with *sh!* written after it. Oh, I know!" Jerry gave Joey a grin.

"Well, what is it?" asked Jock.

"X means a special spot and *sh!* means a secret."

Joey wondered how long it would take Jock to discover the hideaway rock he and Jerry shared now it was marked on the map. But he wanted the map to mean something to all of them, so he put it in. Besides, Jock was the kind who'd see the geology in the rock, not that it was a secret place.

"Where did you find all these names?" asked Mrs. Larkin. "Rabbit Swamp? And Bertie's Boulder? Or Coon-Hunt Woods? and Bulldozed Pond?"

"Those names I made up. Bertie's Boulder is where I found him that day. But the names of the brooks I looked up in that book we have about this whole area from colonial times on. And some of those roads — like East Track — are on real old maps in that book. That's been a path since Indian days, I guess."

"Joe, I'm proud of you." Mr. Larkin got up and shook Joey's hand quite formally. "Congratulations. You are certainly full of surprises."

Joey felt as if such words of praise from his father were king-sized and gift-wrapped.

He let the rest of Christmas — driving down with Jerry to fetch Reino, who, once his holiday shyness wore off, had a fine time; the wonderful dinner; the

171

walk through the woods while Mr. Larkin praised further the well-chosen place names of his map and Reino looked equally proud of Joey; the aunts and uncles and cousins who came for supper; the records played one after another; the games — fall into place about him while he walked through it, aloof in the mantle of his father's appreciation.

As the last cousin flung the final snowball and departed with the last car, Joey realized Bertie hadn't shown up at suppertime.

"I wonder if he's sick from eating all that hamburg last night. Do you suppose he's dying out there somewhere?"

"So that's where the hamburg went!" Mrs. Larkin sounded relieved. "I wondered if I was losing my mind and only thought I bought it."

"Bertie ate it. All but the two last crumbs. He could hardly waddle away. You'll have to watch him now. If you open the refrigerator, he'll climb right in."

"He's probably semi-hibernating, if he ate so much," Jock said.

"I won't worry about him tonight then." Joey went to bed relaxed and happy. His father thought at least something he'd done was good. He fell quickly asleep.

Then suddenly through the drifts and deeps of sleepiness came his father's voice. "Joe! Wake up, Joe!"

"Where are you going off to now?" Joe couldn't seem to unstick his eyelids. "India? Or Brazil?"

"I'm going from Mad to Furious!" Mr. Larkin said loudly. "And you're coming with me. Get your eyes open and get up. Put your bathrobe and shoes on or something. It's your stupid beast."

Joey's heartbeat tripled. "I thought he was so full he'd sleep till tomorrow. What's the matter?"

"He's wide awake and he wants in."

Joe stumbled after his father and then started for the kitchen. "I'll feed him and play with him. You can go back to bed now."

"You come first with me." Mr. Larkin led the way to his bedroom. The lights were not on, but Mrs. Larkin was sitting up in bed, wide awake.

"Joel! Do something, darling. He makes the most ghastly crunching noise — and he won't stop."

Joey listened. He heard sharp strong teeth gnawing outside on the shingles. Two or three crunching noises were followed by a grinding and snapping sound. Then it repeated. Crunch, crunch, grr, snap.

"What is he doing?"

"He is eating the house down," said Mr. Larkin in a voice of icy precision. "He is chewing through and pulling off hand-cut cedar shingles."

Now that Joey's eyes had adjusted, he could see out the window. In the thin wash of moonlight over the snow, he followed Bertie's dark form attacking the gray wall of the house.

"He just needs some food," Joey assured them.

173

"He'd much rather eat hamburg than shingles."

But he took the precaution of placing Bertie's meal all ready on the kitchen floor before he opened the door. If Bertie crunched shingles that angrily he might be in a mood to crunch fingers, too.

He opened the door and called. Bertie walloped across the snow and banged into the house. He didn't even speak to Joey. He ate with great concentration and looked around for more.

Joey sat in a chair with his feet up on the kitchen table. "That's enough food, you pig. You want to be able to waddle, don't you?"

When Bertie found Joey wasn't going to fetch him more food, he rushed across the room and heaved himself onto Joey's lap and placed his front paws on Joey's chest. That brought his glittering black eyes and sharp white teeth extremely close to Joey's nose and caught Joey off balance. Bertie didn't look as if he wanted to play, so Joey tried talking to him.

"What is this? A showdown? You think you have a complaint? It's my parents who have the complaint. What do you mean chewing shingles? That's not only apt to get you thrown out of here, but me, too."

Suddenly Bertie decided to be friendly. He licked Joey's chin. Bertie's tongue was scratchy and he was both rough and thorough with it. Joey's impulse was to pull away, but he didn't dare. In a way this was a showdown with Bertie, and Joey had to come out the master if he was going to be able to keep Bertie around any longer.

Then Bertie collapsed and cuddled against Joey's chest, chirring and wriggling. A small black paw gently patted Joey's face.

"So you're pretending to be nothing but a loving baby again, are you?"

Bertie drew his lips back, distorting his bright face into his silly grin. He made his funny little happy sounds. He never took his eyes off Joey and he never seemed to blink at all.

Joey's grip tightened on him and next thing he knew he was rocking Bertie in his arms. "Why don't you get nice and sleepy, Bertie, and I'll put you outdoors and you go find your house and take a nice long nap. So I can go back to bed. Do you know what time it is, Bertie old boy? The kitchen clock up there says it's two o'clock in the morning and you're not hungry any more and it's bedtime."

Still talking and slowly rocking him, Joey got up and carried him to the kitchen door. He had to move very quickly to open it and shove Bertie out and close it again, but he managed. Bertie stood outside and shrilled crossly.

"Go home!" Joey said loudly and firmly. Bertie ran up and down the steps and banged on the door a few times. Then it was quiet.

"That was a silly thing to tell Bertie," Joey said to

himself. "If this is his home, how can I tell him to go home? I haven't made myself a pet — a friend. All I've done is mix up a perfectly good wild raccoon."

He felt guilty about it. But before he could sort out all his feelings sleep overwhelmed him.

It was a brief sleep. Once again a hand was on his shoulder. This time it was his mother. "Joel, do wake up, dear, and get dressed and take that raccoon far far away. He is under our window again eating shingles and spitting imprecations. We can't stand it one more minute. It's four o'clock in the morning."

"I'm up!" cried Joey, fighting to come awake and slide out of bed. "Where's Dad?"

"He's so mad he's putting his boots on. He says he'll teach Bertie a lesson. That's why you better hurry, dear — "

Joey's grogginess vanished, as Mr. Larkin strode in, a coat flung over his pajamas, a hat jammed on his head, boot laces half-tied and wrath in his eyes. He didn't speak to Joey. He just reached under the bed, hauled out a hockey stick and marched out the door.

"Dad! Wait! I'll stop him — "

Joey stuck his feet into his shoes and ran. Mrs. Larkin ran after him, trying to hand him a coat.

The kitchen door slammed in Joey's face. When he finally pulled it open, his father was racing toward Bertie, the hockey stick raised in the air.

"Don't!" shrieked Joey. "You'll kill him!"

176

"I intend to," Mr. Larkin said furiously. Wielding the hockey stick like a golf club, he swiped viciously at Bertie, with a swing that would have shattered a brittle object to pieces. But there was an evergreen shrub in the way, and the stick, swishing through it, lost some of its force. Even so, Bertie was lifted off balance and plopped into the snow several feet beyond. The noise of the stick whacking his solid body was sickening.

Bertie lay still. Joey turned to his father. "You killed him! Just because you got mad. You wouldn't even let me take care of him!"

"Somebody had to do something, quick!" snapped Mr. Larkin. He dropped the hockey stick and went abruptly into the house.

Joey stood there, stunned. At first he didn't even feel the cold, although he had on just his shoes and the underwear he always slept in. Two things whirled in his mind: he'd lost Bertie; but more than that, he felt as if he'd lost his father. This was a man he didn't know. The other things — the unfinished plans, the untaken trips — he'd tried to understand. But this was too much.

He stood there, shivering, feeling absolutely alone.

7

THERE WAS a whimper from Bertie, and then the animal rolled over. He pushed himself up and shook himself until he staggered.

"Bertie!" Joey hunkered down and slowly put out his hands. "I'm sorry, Bertie. We didn't have a chance — either of us."

Slowly Bertie came to him, and Joey picked him up and held him tight.

"Joel! Come in before you freeze!" Mrs. Larkin called urgently from the back door.

"I can't. I've got Bertie. Dad just stunned him. He didn't kill him after all."

"Oh!" Joey couldn't tell whether his mother's groan was of relief or horror. "Well, you can't just stand there holding him. Come in. Now."

This time Joey didn't hesitate, for he was gasping with cold, but he brought Bertie. Mrs. Larkin shut the door behind him. He kept on holding Bertie. The raccoon's warmth felt so good.

"What can I do?" Joey asked his mother. "Dad will just kill him for sure another time."

"But he didn't mean to kill him this time."

"No? With a swipe like that? Besides, he said he intended to kill him."

"But that was just one of those things you yell when you're mad. He said so, Joey, when he came in. He felt awful about it. He just was so mad he didn't know his own strength. He really will be relieved, Joel, that he didn't kill him."

"I'll believe it if he tells me so and looks me right in the eye."

"I think what you need is some hot tea. You get into bed — "

"With Bertie?"

"Oh, that beastly animal! Joel, he complicates everything. Face it, you will have to get rid of him."

"I know. You don't have to tell me. Chuck my

179

clothes and a blanket and some pillows in here, will you? I'll make myself some tea. I can't throw him out-doors now, because he'll come right back and probably start chewing shingles again."

"I guess you're right," sighed Mrs. Larkin. "We'll have to take care of him in the morning."

When Mrs. Larkin entered the kitchen that morning she found Joey dressed but stretched out on the floor sound asleep. Lying quietly under the blanket, too, was Bertie.

Mrs. Larkin hesitated. Bertie chirruped softly, as if he were telling her not to wake Joey up. Then Bertie crawled out of the blanket and stretched. He seemed gentle and friendly. She watched him lick one of his hind paws, filing his tongue in and out of the long agile fingers, just as if he were washing up for breakfast.

She tried to open the refrigerator door quietly, but Bertie knew the sound. She just slammed it shut with-out having a chance to take anything out as he reached it and growled.

"Joey, wake up!" she begged. "Bertie looks as if he's going to chew right through me to the refrigerator."

"Ummmmm," muttered Joey, sitting up and shaking his head. "I can't move, I'm so tired and stiff! Do you know what Bertie did, even after the way he got bat-tered by a human being last night? He still trusted me enough to put his head down next to mine and just patted me until I fell asleep. He was so warm and good. Mum, do I absolutely have to get rid of him?"

"Absolutely. Irrevocably. And fast."

"You don't think Dad will change his mind, if he's really sorry about last night? *If.*"

"Have you looked at the outside of the house?"

Joey pulled himself to his feet and stared out the window. Drizzle dripped through fog. Snow on the ground wept into puddles and ran away wherever it could. But through the gloom Joey could see the white scars of ripped shingles on the bedroom wing of the house.

"Each time it sounded as if one more bite and his teeth would stick right through the wall into our room. We couldn't sleep."

"I'm sorry, Mum. I wish I knew what to do."

They both stared at Bertie, who rolled on his back on the floor, playing with a ball of fluff he'd found under the refrigerator.

"Dad probably wants me to march him out like a prisoner this morning and have Reino shoot him as if he were a mad red squirrel. Well, I won't. I'll phone the nearest zoo and see if they'll take him. But he'd hate being in a cage."

"Why don't you take him off and leave him in the woods?"

"Do you suppose he'd find food? Or would he starve looking for raisins and Ritz crackers? I guess I haven't been very smart or very kind to him after all."

181

Joey slumped into a seat at the table. It didn't help when Bertie wandered over and leaned against him and put a hand confidentially on his knee. He stared up at Joey, as if he really were trying to understand what his friend worried so about.

Jock came in. "What's he doing in here now? And what was all the noise last night?"

"Bertie and Dad had a disagreement," Mrs. Larkin said briefly. "And I wouldn't mention it to Dad this morning. Jock, what's the name of that zoo near Stoneham?"

Joey leaned over Bertie and asked very seriously, "Would you like it in a cold smelly cement square with iron bars and millions of people staring at you? Could you stand it?"

"Why don't you call the Trailside Museum? There's one beyond Boston," Jock suggested. "They have animals that are used to kids and they don't keep them in cages all the time. I just read about it in a magazine."

"Speaking of magazines, Jock," said Mrs. Larkin, "Your shelves are a fire hazard. I hope we don't ever have to empty the fish tank over them to put out the flames."

"I'll straighten them up. If I can ever get to the table and eat my breakfast."

"You'll have breakfast if I can open the refrigerator door," Mrs. Larkin promised. "Aren't you going to put Bertie outdoors, Joel?"

"I thought you wanted me to get rid of him. If I put him out, then he'll go away. He may not come back till the middle of the night. And that's not the best time to start out for any zoo or museum."

But every time his mother tried to open the refrigerator, Bertie made a dash for it. When Joey tried to hold him back, Bertie struggled. Finally he nipped Joey's finger and drew blood.

"That does it," Mrs. Larkin cried. "Put him out right now."

"He didn't mean to bite *me*," Joey tried to explain. "He was just annoyed at my hand holding him back."

"I don't need an interpreter," said Mrs. Larkin, "and I worry about bites and rabies and all kinds of things. You see, Joel, this is a ridiculous situation. Bertie is not a real pet, because he goes off to the woods all the time. You don't know who he hangs around with out there."

Joey burst out laughing. He couldn't help it. And then Mrs. Larkin laughed, too.

"I know it sounds nutty, worrying about who he hangs around with out there. But what I mean is that it's an uncontrolled situation with no safeguards. If he were continually caged and you always knew what his health was and what animals were near him, that would be different."

"That's true," Joey admitted. "But remember how he climbed out of the cage every night? He didn't want to be a caged pet. He wants freedom to run in the woods and then come see us if he chooses to. I think that's a great relationship to have with a wild animal. It means we're friends."

"Yes — but on his terms. And that's where the trouble comes. When he's in our environment, he should live on our terms, not his."

"Why?" asked Joey. "Why does everything always have to be on *our* terms? Is there always just one way to do something? Why can't people be different?"

"You're talking about being a non-comformist," Jock told him.

"I don't care what you call it. I just know I don't want to act like everybody else just because I'm supposed to. I'm me and I want to be me — in any way I need to."

"That's what Bertie is probably saying to himself," Mrs. Larkin pointed out. "He wants to do whatever he wants to when he needs to, no matter how it affects anyone else. And see what happens? Chaos. Joel, run that finger under the faucet and give it a good wash with soap."

Joey moved to the sink and turned on the faucet. In a flash Bertie scaled the slippery kitchen cabinets, slid across the counter top and sat by the sink. He reached for the water and tried to wash his hands, too.

"Conformist!" Joey screeched at him. "All these months you haven't washed a drop of your food the way raccoons are supposed to. And now you rush up here and wash your hands just like me. I suppose you think there'll be faucets out in the woods."

He shut off the stream of water, leaving an occasional drip. Bertie tried to catch the drips. Then he dropped into the sink and sat under the faucet, hopefully opening his mouth for a drink.

Mrs. Larkin quickly pulled the refrigerator door open and grabbed out eggs, butter, milk and juice.

Bertie picked up the squeeze bottle of a dish-washing liquid. He squeezed and tiny pink bubbles floated up in the air. He dropped the bottle to reach for the bubbles.

"Jock, run get my camera quick!" said Mrs. Larkin. "What a picture that would make."

Joey squeezed more bubbles for Bertie to catch, while Mrs. Larkin snapped pictures. They were as busy as a photographer's studio when Mr. Larkin stepped in to find out what had happened to his breakfast.

"Final souvenir snaps?" he asked. "Then you should at least have one or two of Joe holding the surly creature."

"I suppose so," said Mrs. Larkin. "Could you hold him still long enough, Joel?"

Joey picked Bertie out of the sink and put him on his shoulder. For just a few seconds Bertie swung into his favorite position — one hind leg around each side of Joey's neck, his front paws in Joey's hair and his own eager face bobbing above Joey's head.

Mrs. Larkin worked fast. "There, those should be wonderful. Now, you'd better put him out so I can cook and you can phone."

With Mr. Larkin seated hungrily at the kitchen table, Joey didn't argue. Nor did he want any flare-up of temper on his father's part or disturbance on Bertie's. He carried him out and stood on the back steps, watching as the raccoon stepped through the slushy snow out of sight around the house. Joey waited a bit and then tiptoed sloppily after him. Bertie's tracks led over the lawn, toward the brook, but Bertie was not in view. Joey still had no idea where the coon holed up.

Joey finally phoned the Trailside Museum and talked to a Mr. Garrett. When he returned to the kitchen, Jerry was there, and his mother was cooking piles of pancakes.

"They can't take him at the Museum," Joey reported. "They already have two raccoons and are about to turn them loose. He guesses Bertie would be just about their age — about nine months old. He says they get stronger and nippier and less lovable as they grow older."

"Bertie could hardly be less lovable than he is right now," said Mr. Larkin. Joey waited, hoping his father would at least say he was sorry for his attack on the raccoon. Joey thought he could understand and even forgive his father if he'd just say he was sorry. But he didn't.

186

"Anyway," Joey went on, "Mr. Garrett said now is the perfect time to release him because he's old enough to fend for himself, but young enough to adapt to his real environment. And he says that since Bertie has holed up outside anyway it won't be a hard adjustment. So he says to take him away — about four or five miles — to a swampy place and let him go."

"I'll drive you right now, gladly!" announced Mr. Larkin. "Let's go."

"I had to put him out so you could eat," Joey reminded him. "And he's wandered off to wherever he holes up. So we'll have to wait till the next time he comes to the house."

"It better not be at two o'clock in the morning," said Mr. Larkin. "Or I'll finish the job right there."

Joey stared at Mrs. Larkin. Maybe his father hadn't felt sorry at all, and his mother just said he did to make Joey feel better. She started to say something but the phone rang. "That's my call." Mr. Larkin left the room.

"Have some pancakes," Mrs. Larkin urged Joey.

He shook his head. "I'm too tired to chew."

Joey went back to bed and slept until noon. Then he decided to find Bertie and ask his father to drive them off to the woods, rather than take a chance on another bad night. He put on his raincoat and rubber boots. The tracks Bertie had left that morning were sloshed away, but Joey walked up and down the brook, listening and calling. Except for the rushing gurgle of the brook and the slurpy sound his boots made, it was quiet. Wherever Bertie was, if he heard he chose not to reply.

Bertie did not come at supper time, which was just as well, as the drizzle and fog turned to a drenching rain. Joey went to bed braced for being awakened at any hour by an irate father reporting attack by raccoon. It amazed him to wake up to the drumming of rain on the roof and see that it was already nine o'clock. No one was in the kitchen, so Joey fried himself an egg and ate it with ketchup and cheese. Mrs. Larkin found him staring out the window.

"This would have been the vacation to go to New York and spend all the days indoors," she said.

"Bertie didn't try to chew the house down last night?"

"Not a sound. But I hope he shows up so we can solve this before your father leaves the day after New Year's. He's on the phone trying to schedule things now."

"Where is he going?"

"Back to Scotland. Same place, but different problem."

Joey felt a flash of fear race through his stomach. "Did he say anything more about me and that school?"

"No. He said he'd wait till your mid-year marks. You know once he decides something he doesn't go back over it again. He's much too involved about the right machinery for his problem with the plastics."

There was a sharp tap on the back door, followed by an impatient chittering.

"It's Bertie!" Joey quickly filled Bertie's bowl and set it on the floor. Somehow when he let the raccoon in, he expected Bertie would explain where he'd been. It was frustrating when Bertie just waddled grumpily over to his dish without any kind of greeting.

"I'll go alert Dad that the Transportation and Rehabilitation Committee can get to work," said Mrs. Larkin. "Want me to bring your raincoat and boots in here for you?"

"Can't you even let him eat before you rush him out the door?" Joey asked crossly.

"I'm sorry. You want to be left alone with him for a while? To say goodby?"

"Oh, Mum! Do you have to be sentimental, too?"

"No," said Mrs. Larkin. "I don't *have* to be anything but your mother. Which gets more difficult every day." She hurried out of the kitchen.

Bertie ate everything in his dish. Then he climbed the cupboards and up onto the counter. His busy paws spilled the sugar and mangled a tangerine before he decided he wasn't crazy about the taste of either. Then he strolled into the sink and turned the faucet on so he could have a drink. Joey made a quick dash across the kitchen to turn it off. Bertie hissed angrily.

"If you're that smart, you'll have to learn to read Hot and Cold, too," Joey said. "I shut it off because it was hot. In another minute you'd have scalded your tonsils."

Mr. Larkin walked in carrying Joey's outdoor things. "I'll bring the truck to the kitchen door. Then we'll pop him in and take him off before he can escape. All right?"

Joey nodded. He wished his father would talk about the hockey-stick episode. He didn't dare bring it up, but he felt it was a soundproof glass wall between them.

Mr. Larkin strode out.

Joey set the cold water faucet so the drops spilled out slowly and kept Bertie busy trying to catch them. Then he pulled on the rubber boots and old storm coat. When Mr. Larkin honked, Joey reached for the raccoon.

Bertie saw him coming. Perhaps it was only because the sink was slippery, but he held up his front paws like a baby waiting to be picked up. When Joey hugged him, he seemed to hug back.

"Don't you dare lick me," whispered Joey, as he opened the back door. "Don't you dare be good buddies right now." He just made it into the front seat of the cab beside his father, before the raccoon struggled free.

Bertie braced himself against Joey's chest as the jeep pulled out of the driveway and along the narrow road. "Where are you going?"

190

"How about Carlson's Swamp? That place your mother likes to go for cat-o'-nine-tails. It's far enough away from houses so Bertie wouldn't run back to civilization and be a garbage bum."

"It's a trafficky twisty turny enough trip so he'd never be able to find his way back," Joey said flatly.

"Is that what's in the back of your mind? That he'll come back to you?"

"Well, I know in my mind he won't. Only heroic cats and dogs in the movies and on TV do that." He couldn't admit that in his heart he hoped Bertie would come back to see him. To prove they were really friends. But should it ever happen, he also hoped his father would be far away!

"If he knows what's good for him, he'll take to the woods and like it," said Mr. Larkin.

Bertie did not enjoy the ride. The truck snorted and smelled of unwoods-like fumes. Other cars whizzed wetly by. When Bertie tried to hold onto the windshield, his paws slipped down the glass and he banged his head. He clawed his way onto Joey's shoulder and kept waving his tail in Joey's eyes.

The truck banged past the path to the rocks where Joey lost the rabbit. Once Bertie had come into his life, he'd almost forgotten that rabbit. Now only a few ducks swam in the cove and one sea gull perched sullenly on a rock.

"This is such rotten weather there isn't any stormy surf to watch or driftwood to look for," complained Joey.

They drove away from the immediate shoreline with its boarded-up summer houses and through the small village of Dove Cove. Houses strung out on each side of the route until they turned onto a road that climbed a steep hill. There were only a few dwellings. As the road became a dirt track, woods and underbrush closed it in.

Mr. Larkin drove to where the road quit, and luckily there was room to back around. He backed.

"Well, Joey?"

Now the moment had come, Joey couldn't bear the burden of it. He just sat there, waiting for his father to become impatient. After all, he was the one who hated Bertie — let him be the executioner. Then Bertie solved the problem. He pawed at the glass and seemed eager to get out.

"Open the door," Mr. Larkin said. "Let him go by himself."

Joey opened the door. Bertie scrambled from the seat to the floor of the cab and sat staring out.

"He looks like a paratrooper making up his mind to jump," said Mr. Larkin. "Go ahead, Bertie! Geronimo! The swamp is just beyond those trees."

Bertie scrambled out. Hesitantly he picked his way

192

over the mud to where browned and beaten oak leaves were wind-piled by a bush.

For one second he looked back over his fat furry shoulder — his bright eyes unblinking.

Then at an unhurried pace, as if he were a dignified banker out for a noontime stroll, Bertie walked into the underbrush, his beautiful tail floating behind him.

"Well, there he goes. Off to a life of no responsibilities. I envy him," Mr. Larkin decided. "He won't have to be entertaining and lovable when he isn't in the mood. And he won't have to explain anything he does on the impulse to another living soul."

Joey grunted. It was as close as his father had come to mentioning his attack on Bertie. But no apology followed.

Mr. Larkin drove slowly out of the small clearing, and began talking about many different things, as if words could quickly fill the space left empty by one overstuffed, unreliable, ridiculous raccoon.

Joey didn't even bother to answer. At home he walked into the library and shut the door. He sat in a chair and stared out the window at the rain. After half an hour his mother came in with hot cocoa for him.

"Don't be sad, Joel. You had to do it. But don't dwell on it."

"I'm not dwelling on it. I just feel as if I didn't have anything to do any more."

"Bertie was time-consuming. You'll be free now to do lots of things."

"Like what? This time of year you can't even send me out to weed the garden to keep me busy."

"You could read some books. You could take up the guitar — you could — "

Joey interrupted impatiently. "Even though it's a disgrace to say so in this house, I don't care that much about reading. You know what? You think everybody has to be doing something constructive all the time. And I should be satisfied with packaged time-fillers or something. Like a book. Or a kit to make something. Well, I don't work that way. You can't buy me an Instant-Do-Something and expect me to be happy. Don't I have a right to be unhappy if I want to? Do I always have to be smiling, busy and doing the right thing all the time — like Dad!"

Mrs. Larkin put the cocoa down with a bang, but she knew Joey lashed out because he was feeling very sorry for himself. And she knew there wasn't anything to say right then that would make him feel better. The dignity of silence seemed best.

But when she left, she didn't pull the door shut tightly enough, and it drifted open behind her. Joey heard her say, "Rory, I think we've made the most terrible mistake in our whole lives. Somehow or other we should have managed it so Joel didn't have to give up that raccoon."

194

"Ruth, you're crazy. That raccoon was a menace."

"Well, we did lose some sleep one night. But did we really give Joey a chance to work out the problem for himself? You know, you can be just a little high-handed when you feel impatient about things."

"I'm glad you call my taking a swing at that beast just a little high-handed. Joey called it attempted murder, I'm sure."

"Did you talk to him about it?"

"No. You know I don't like to get into emotional discussions — especially with the kids."

"But they don't understand you sometimes. All you need to do is explain and be sympathetic."

"Tush!" said Mr. Larkin. "We've had too much of parents being made accountable to their children. It should still be the other way around, the way it was when my father brought me up. I was solely responsible for my own actions, and accountable to him until I was an adult. He didn't allow excuses, and I don't either, for myself or anyone else. Now if we've made a mistake about Joey and his raccoon, then we'll all have to make the best of it."

"Just this once, I wish I was the one who was leaving. I'd gladly go to Scotland for any length of time!"

"There's an idea. Come with me, Ruth! I need you as much as the boys do. Get Della or that Mrs. Grumpit or whatever her name is who advertises that she Accommodates Young People. Get one of them to stay with Jock and Joe, and run away with me."

Joey, listening from the library, wished desperately his mother had closed the door. But the voices went on. He couldn't escape them.

"I couldn't go now, Rory. It really would be walking out on Joel at a terrible time."

"Oh, he'll get over the raccoon, Ruth. Why, there was a dog I mourned. When he died I thought life would never be the same again. And now I can't remember if he was a combination Collie-Doberman or a Collie-Dalmation. Joe has just got to learn that life isn't going to go his way all the time."

"That's what worries me. Life never seems to go his way. It goes our way, yours or mine or Jerry's or Jock's. We're all consumed by our self-interests that we pursue with such enthusiasm, and Joel just gets left out."

"Then let him find his own enthusiasms and pursue them."

"He did. It was Bertie."

"You know that was an impossible situation to continue. You told him yourself he'd have to get rid of him. Bertie became a destructive animal."

"Oh, I'm just as much to blame in the things I said and the lack of real thought I gave the problem. But I don't think you can say that Bertie deliberately became a destructive animal. He became a bewildered animal — bewildered by a highly complicated way

196

of life he was never designed to fit into. Just the way Joel is a bewildered boy."

Joey jumped from his chair and started to the door. He couldn't bear to hear any more about himself. It hurt too much, as if he were watching himself being operated on by a team of surgeons all with different ideas as to what ailed him. But even while he watched, bewildered, he could feel the pain.

"Ruth, stop getting all bawled up in pseudo-psychology and guilty feelings. Try positive thinking, for heaven's sake! A strong constructive attitude around him will help buck Joey up. Don't worry. No child of ours will be a blot on either family escutcheon — yours or mine. There's too much quality and background poured into that boy."

Joey wasn't sure what an escutcheon was, but the words *blot* and *family* bobbed about in his mind as he shut the door. "The Family Blot. That's what I am for sure. Just the good old Family Blot."

In a way it was a relief to have some title for himself. When his father came in a few minutes later and said, "Put your coat on. We're taking your map into town and order a frame for it," Joey agreed to go. He had suddenly found a role for himself, and since he was too confused to fight it, he'd fit it.

On New Year's Eve, the family was considerate. No one once mentioned Bertie. His mother had picked up Bertie's dish, boiled it, and put it away. Reino had re-

197

placed the ripped shingles. Even his own souvenirs of Bertie's teeth, the scars on his hands, began to fade away.

The rains finally stopped. Cold blasts of air from Canada swept down and the wishy-washy ice on the pond hardened at last. Joey phoned his friends and on New Year's Day they had a marathon hockey game. For the first time in the forty-eight hours since Bertie was removed, Joey was too busy to think of him. He came in to supper that night exhausted but glowing.

"Anyone want to play Monopoly?" he asked. It was family tradition at some time on New Year's Day to play Monopoly, with a lot of laughter about a good year ahead for the winner and the losers better be prudent.

"I'm all packed and organized," Mr. Larkin said, "so I'll play. How about you, Jerry? Are you all set to drive to the airport and fly off to New York with me tomorrow?"

"Tomorrow?" Jerry frowned. "I thought maybe I'd take a train the next day. I don't have to check in until ten that night. I'm not in that much of a rush to leave home, Dad. I'd rather have one more quiet day here in the woods."

"I didn't think you were that much of a nature boy," said Mr. Larkin in surprise. But Jerry kept his face impassive.

"It wouldn't do Jerry any harm to have one more

day at home. He still looks as if he didn't eat enough. Is the food at the school that poor? Or are you just working it all off on the piano?"

"Oh, the food's all right, Mum." Jerry shrugged. "But nothing to get excited about. Just don't fuss."

Mrs. Larkin started to ask Jerry something else, when Mr. Larkin interrupted. "Where's that Monopoly game? If Jerry starts one of his all-or-nothing wars with me, we'll be up all night."

But the game broke up by ten-thirty, with Mrs. Larkin feeling cheerful because she won — a rare occasion. "Maybe this will be a good year after all!"

No one had time in the morning to discuss omens of good or bad fortune. It was all rush and bustle.

"Remember your Christmas Eve resolutions about studying, Joe," said Mr. Larkin. "If I'm not home, Mum will cable me your marks at mid-years. And don't take in any more stray animals."

"I was thinking of trying something more my type. A porcupine."

"Joe!" Mr. Larkin flung an arm around his shoulders. "You're making me feel like an ogre. Do I look like an ogre this morning?"

Joe stared at his father. They were almost eye-to-eye now in height. But his father's body always seemed to give off the feeling of superb tensile strength, just as his mind could send out brain waves of energetic conviction. In the brittle white sunlight, outlined against the glittering ice which rimed trees and grass, his father seemed as dazzling, as unconquerable and overwhelming as he had when Joey was a little boy. Joey wanted to forget the man he had seen, white with anger, the hockey stick flashing in his hand.

"Take care of your mother for me." Mr. Larkin squeezed Joey's shoulder, hurried to the car with Mrs. Larkin and Jock, and off he charged.

It was bitter cold out, but Joey's friends agreed to come and play hockey on the pond. For three hours the screech of skates, clash of sticks and general screaming and yelling woke up the still woods. Blue jays and crows flapped away huffily. Dogs who had followed the boys growled and yelped at a particularly cross squirrel, scolding at all the noise in his front yard.

By dusk, when Joey finally came in, the house was filled with tremendous quiet. Without his father's quick step, the whole atmosphere seemed dead. He suddenly realized that Jerry hadn't touched the piano all vacation either, except the first night when his father made him play. He wondered if his parents were aware of it, or if they had been too busy, too distracted by Joey's problems and Jock's projects and Bertie's behavior to notice.

There was absolutely nothing to do except study, and Joey wouldn't do that on general principles because vacation wasn't over until the next morning.

How welcome Bertie's rudest snort of demand would be.

"Let's eat in the kitchen tonight," said his mother. "I'm tired. Fussing around in the dining room is too much bother."

"Sure," said Joey. "The nearer the refrigerator, the better."

Jerry was unusually silent, but Jock chattered away as they ate, and once Joey stopped chewing and listened.

"What's the matter?"

"Nothing. Thought I heard the back door rattle. Probably just the wind."

After supper Joey couldn't seem to settle down to anything. His mother growled at him when she saw him watching an old Western on TV. "Honestly, Joel, you've seen something like that hundreds of times. You know just what's going to happen. How can you bear to waste the time?"

"How many times have you heard the same symphony over and over?"

"That's different. You always discover something new each time you hear it — some new meaning or feeling. You're not wasting time, you're learning. Or if you're not listening intellectually, you're listening emotionally and it can be either an uplifting or a relaxing experience."

"But I'm learning something new. These cowboys are from a different ranch and these Indians are a different tribe than I've seen before. And I'm enjoying a relaxing experience. Is there anything wrong with that?"

"If you argue it that way, Joel, it sounds as if nothing were wrong. But it is wrong, because it's a stupid waste of time."

"No. It would be wrong for you, because you like different things. You like music. I like TV."

"Just wait till your mid-year marks come in, Joel, and then we'll argue. We'll see just where this wasted winter of TV watching and raccoon-sitting has left you."

But he realized his mother couldn't settle down to anything either. She'd be restless until Dad cabled "Landed okay" from Scotland.

He switched off the TV. "I thought if I argued with you, it would keep your mind off Dad."

"Oh, you!"

"Do you want to play Scrabble? Not that I'm any good at it." This was a real sacrifice on his part. He usually avoided the game because the rest of the family was so brilliant at it. But that little bit of overheard conversation about his mother wishing she could go away on a trip with his father made him feel sorry for her right now.

"Would you?" She was pleased, so he found the

game and set up the table. "You know, Joel, we always seem to be scolding you or hammering at you about something. And yet you're the one who is the most understanding. The rest of us get so stupidly busy." She looked at him lovingly.

"Oh, Mum. Don't get sloppy."

"Do you think Jerry would like to play? I don't hear him practicing."

Joey started to say, "Maybe Jerry isn't all that keen on music after all," when he remembered his brother had warned him not to say anything.

"Maybe he's packing," Joey suggested. "Or sleeping. He said he had a lot of sleep to catch up on."

"I know," Mrs. Larkin worried. "He was exhausted when he came home, although he won't admit it. I must remember to put some vitamin pills in his suitcase. If I didn't know he loved the piano so much, I'd wonder if something were really wrong with him. I guess he's just working too hard."

It was a long game, and Joey tried not to fidget. He was relieved when it ended, even if his mother did win by ninety points.

"I'll lock up," he told her.

"Good. Be sure to set your alarm for school tomorrow."

Joey groaned. It was always tough to start again after the holidays. And it would be twice as hard for Jerry, feeling the way he did. Joey realized Jerry might be asleep when he left for school in the morning and have left for New York before he returned. He went down to the Music Room to say goodby.

Jerry was sitting in a large chair, reading. He didn't even have music going on the record player. Such complete quiet made the room seem cold and uncomfortable.

"Why don't you read up in the library where it's warmer?" asked Joey.

"I like the quiet," said Jerry and went on looking at his book.

"I can take a hint. But I did want to say goodby and good luck."

"Thanks for the luck bit." Jerry managed a small smile. "I'll need it. So will you, I guess. Mum told me two flunks and you are on the next plane to Scotland."

"That's right. So just remember if you feel glum at the Conservatory that at least you don't have to take cold showers and wear knee socks."

Jerry looked at him and shivered.

"You feel all right?" Joey asked. "I mean — Mum was worried about your needing vitamins or something."

"No, I don't feel all right." Jerry slammed the book shut. "But vitamins won't help. I went to a doctor in New York because I thought maybe my fingers weren't strong enough after all that business last summer. But he said there was nothing wrong with me physically. So I have no excuses at all."

"But you're still worried about playing the piano?"

"No. Not about playing the piano!" Jerry said in acid tones. "Anybody — you or Reino — can *play the piano*. I am concerned about being a pianist."

"Oh." Joey said it meekly because he could see Jerry was getting worked up over it. "Anyway, good luck. When are you coming home again? Do you get a spring vacation?"

"I may be home long before then. Permanently."

Joey shrugged. He knew just how Jerry felt. It wouldn't matter if anyone contradicted him, or tried to give him a pep talk. As long as Jerry felt that way, he wouldn't hear what anyone else said. But he didn't have to feel all alone about it, the way Joey usually did.

"Jerry, if I can help you any time, will you let me know? You could write me. Or call me up, you know. If you need to."

For a moment the old sparkle flashed in Jerry's eyes. "Old Faithful Joe. The Find-It, Fix-It Kid. Well, don't sit around waiting. But thanks anyway."

He opened the book again.

Joey went up the stairs. Just as he reached the door, Jerry called, "Wait, Joey! I'm sorry you had to take Bertie away. At least for a while he was the only thing around here that Dad couldn't run his way."

"Yeah," said Joey. "It was fun while it lasted."

205

8

CRISP AND COLD the January days clanked by — iced in by frozen journeys to and from school, and filled only by the rigid demands of studying. Joey suddenly made up his mind. He would pass math and French. He would do better in his other courses. He would take no chance on being sent to a foreign school. He studied until his mind ached, as he painfully reached for understanding.

He didn't mention Bertie. Even his secret wish for Bertie's return was tamped into the bottom of his mind, and when two weeks and then three went by without a familiar bang at the door, or a paw print in the snow near the house, Joey sadly dismissed his hope. Reino kept the paths shoveled and the woodpiles stacked and stopped in the house for coffee each afternoon to see if there were any letters from Mr. Larkin about jobs Reino should do.

"This is the worst time of year," Mrs. Larkin complained. "Sometimes I wish I could hibernate and wake up when it's over."

"Just getting from one day to the next is a real chore," Reino agreed. "But you come out and take a walk in the woods with me on the next sunny day. The twigs in the swamps are turning pink, and the pussy willows are coming out. You can see spring is all there waiting."

"That's what I hate," said Joey. "Just *waiting*. I've got three exams next week spread all the way over Monday and Tuesday. And then two long days of waiting, with both my worst exams on the last day. Friday."

"Both math and French on Friday?" asked his mother.

"Right. What a schedule."

"At least you'll have the others off your mind and two extra days to study," she pointed out.

"You can help me out in the woods those days," Reino grinned. "Good hard work. Give your mind a break. Clear up the fog."

"I may do that. My mind feels like a soggy sponge

that is not going to absorb one bit more by Friday."

But on Wednesday, Joey was still trying. He spent the day in his room, with his math book, because he had a little more hope of passing that than the French. Part way through the afternoon, Mrs. Larkin knocked on his door.

"I just had a thought, Joel! I'm going to the library. What if I borrow some French language records for you to listen to? Would that help?"

"Thanks, Mum, but I'm afraid it would mix me up more. If I heard a real French French accent after two years of a down-Maine-and-false-teeth French accent, I wouldn't understand anything at all."

"Well. I'll see if they have any. Just in case you change your mind."

Exhausted by his lonely battle with the new math and the final humiliation of having to ask Jock, who had already had two years of it in school, to help him, Joey slept late Thursday morning. Mrs. Larkin finally woke him up.

"If you're going to conquer your French today, you'd better be up and at it."

"Oh, all right. It might do me just as much good to work with Reino today and listen to Finnish."

"But you'll do well on these exams, Joel!" Mrs. Larkin sounded genuinely convinced. "I've never seen you study so hard. By the way, I did borrow those French records, but if you want to listen to them, you'll have to use the record player in the Music Room. The one in the living room needs to be fixed."

As Joey dressed, he decided what he needed most was fresh air. "I'm going to work with Reino after all. I'll take a sandwich and be back around two," Joey told his mother.

It was a beautiful day in the woods. Joey spent a busy hour clipping the lower branches from the pines. Soon he and Reino were surrounded with a carpet of pungent green slash. It felt good to sit on a log and eat his sandwich, while he enjoyed even the feeble touch of faded winter sun on his face.

"Were you still going to school when you were fifteen, Reino?"

"No. I had to help my mother by the time I was twelve. I cut hay and milked the cow and chopped wood. The only people in our village who kept on to school were a boy who wanted to be a pastor and another who wanted to teach. No one else could take the time."

"Maybe that's the way it ought to be here. Unless you really want to go on — for some good reason like teaching — you shouldn't. It would save an awful lot of time and money."

"No." Reino shook his head. "It would make more and more poor people and a poor country. You just have to have all the education you can to get ahead nowadays."

The unexpected crunch of footsteps in the snow startled them. It was Mrs. Larkin, rosy-faced from hurrying.

"Mum! Anything wrong?"

"No. I just had a surprise overseas phone call from Dad. He's flying to New York to a company briefing he must attend for three days. And then he's going to rush from New York right off to Brazil. He wants me to take a plane down tonight and meet him at his hotel — stay with him while he's there. Otherwise it will be weeks before he sees any of us again. We can look up Jerry tomorrow and I do feel anxious about him. He hasn't written since he went back. So I came to see if Reino would be willing to stay at the house with you and Jock until Monday."

"I'll be glad to, Mrs. Larkin. It's easier than hiking back and forth in this weather."

"Thank you, Reino. I can drive you home now to pick up anything you need. And Joel, I'm sorry to leave you with your two exams tomorrow. But there's nothing I really could do to help you with them."

"That's all right, Mum." Joey tried not to feel let down. After all, what could she do tomorrow beside stoke him with a good breakfast and wish him luck? "I guess Dad and Jerry need you more this time."

By supper time she was off to catch a plane, and Joey, Jock and Reino settled comfortably into an all-male household. During the evening Joey's conscience caught up with him and he took the French records down to the Music Room. He lit a fire in the fireplace and turned the heat way up, but the room was really cold from not being used since Christmas vacation. So he sat on the floor in a huddle of blankets and tried to concentrate on the records. Over and over he listened, until the sound became sheer monotony and put him to sleep.

He woke with a great start, to find someone standing by him.

"Reino! I'm ready to quit and go to bed."

"I'm not Reino." Joey's sleepiness vanished. It was Jerry's voice.

"Where's Mum? This is the only lighted room in the whole house."

"It's lucky you didn't go into her room to wake her up, because Reino's sleeping in there. Mum's in New York. Say — she went down to meet Dad and see you! What are you doing here?"

"I came home to see her," Jerry said flatly. "Missing her is par for the course, I guess. Like everything else lately. What are you doing down here?"

"I was trying to study for my French exam. It's at nine o'clock tomorrow morning. But I fell asleep."

"You're lucky you can sleep." Jerry stood out of the lamplight, so Joey couldn't clearly see his face. But he sounded even more tired and discouraged than he had at Christmas. Things must be much worse, Joey

211

thought, if Jerry had to come home to talk to Mum.

"What'll you do now? Go back to New York and see Mum there? I can tell you where she and Dad are staying."

"No. I want to talk to her alone. Before I see Dad. I just want to make up my mind, write my speech, memorize it, and go in and recite it to Dad — without interruptions and arguments. And then go off somewhere."

"You're quitting the Conservatory?"

"I am. But I wanted to tell Mum why, because she'd listen. Dad would hear the words all right. But I don't think he'd understand what I really said."

"You might as well stay here until she comes home then. Dad's going from New York right to Brazil."

"Good." Jerry took his coat off and poked up the fire. "You look absolutely groggy, Joey. You ought to go to bed."

"I'm on my way." But in the hallway Joey stumbled over Lancelot, and the dog, seeing someone who could let him out, went to the front door and barked.

"Honestly, Lancelot, do you have to go out now? Make it a short trip, will you?" Joey yawned. He stood in the doorway for a few minutes, feeling the raw winds of the winter night probe down his neck and up his sleeves. Then he whistled. But Lancelot didn't come.

Joey groaned. He shut the door and, being thoroughly awakened by the cold, decided to make himself cocoa and a sandwich. By that time Lancelot would be banging at the door. He found the peanut butter and grape jelly and popped four slices of bread in the toaster. There was a scratch at the back door. He hurried to let Lancelot in.

But when he opened the door, the dog did not charge through. Nothing happened, except for a moan from the wind.

"Lancelot! You oaf! Come in here."

No bark. No scatter of paws on the crusted snow. No rushing sounds from the dark.

Yet there was something. Joey stood there, a small finger of warning seeming to press an alarm in his brain. Something was there in the pitch-black night.

Joey switched on the outside light and looked down. There lying inert on the doorstep, his eyes open but somehow unseeing, was a raccoon.

"Bertie!" Joey scooped him up and took him into the bright warmth of the kitchen. He knew it was Bertie — but what could his beautiful friend have gone through in four weeks?

Not only was the silver glow faded, but he weighed pounds less. And his paws! The soft pads of both his front and hind feet were scratched and bleeding. On the inside of his tail, half of which fell over at almost a right angle, was a large raw wound.

"Look what I did to him!" Joey spoke out loud, as

if he were an actor beginning a soliloquy. But he didn't feel like an actor. He felt the live coals of anguish inside himself. "Look what I did to him — and he still came home."

What could he do to help him now? Not much more than put him into a cardboard box with old pieces of blanket and see what warmth and rest would do.

As soon as Lancelot returned, Joey carried the box to his room. Bertie didn't even open his eyes when Joey put the box down as gently as he could. During the night Joey woke and turned on the light several times. Bertie hadn't moved at all.

After seven the sun rose with a cold steel-like glitter and stabbed Joey awake. He looked at the clock and groaned. In an hour he would have to start running for the bus and his nine o'clock exam. The house was absolutely still. He took the box to the kitchen and saw from the rinsed coffee cup and plate that Reino was already up, breakfasted and outdoors.

After he ate, Joey roused Bertie and tried to spoon a little warm milk into him. But beyond opening his eyes and twitching his ears and swallowing about two spoonfuls, the raccoon made no attempt to move.

Joey stared at him with an overwhelming sadness. Was it fair to nurse Bertie back to health — if he could — only to have his father return and either kill him or make Joey take him away again? It was hardly fair to put him out in the woods now, helpless, where the cold

214

or a wild animal would finish him off. Joey had created this situation and he had to solve it by some choice of action.

Of course he could be a coward and hand the box to Reino and say, "Take him away and don't tell me what you do with him." He remembered how Reino had refused to make friends with Bertie and said, "You'll need someone someday who doesn't love him."

Or he could wait until his mother came back and say, "Please ask the vet to put him to sleep." But he knew his mother would suffer over it.

Yet his immediate problem, he realized with dismay, was to get to school for those exams. He couldn't even take the time now to reason out what to do. He'd have to wake up Jerry and ask him to keep Bertie in a warm place and spoon some milk into him every hour or so.

Just then he heard footsteps in the glass-enclosed passage that led from the Music Room to the kitchen. But they didn't come through. Instead the outside door from the passage to the terrace banged.

If Jerry had gone out for some reason, Joey would have to leave him Bertie and a note. And whatever he did must be quick. With no ride to the bus, he'd have to leave the house in ten minutes. He couldn't afford to be late to that exam.

He hurried to the Music Room. No one was there. The tumble of blankets on the couch looked as if a tornado had slept there. But the stacks of music, usually strewn over the top of the piano, were piled neatly. Jerry couldn't have changed his mind and left for a return train or plane to New York because his suitcase, partly unpacked, lay open on a table.

It looked as if Jerry had spent a sleepless night and decided to go out for a walk to revive himself. Joey decided to leave Bertie's box in the kitchen where someone would be sure to see it. So he ran back and left it on the table with a note. "Keep Bertie warm. Try warm milk with spoon every hour or so. I'll be home about four P.M. Joe."

After he wrote the note, he realized that something about the empty Music Room was bothering him. Almost against his will, he was drawn back to the top of the stairs by something that insistently caught at his mind. What was different, besides the neatly stacked music?

Then he saw that the piano keyboard was covered by its wooden lid. He couldn't ever remember seeing the piano closed up like that. It was like seeing a coffin shut at a funeral. Since he had come home last night, Jerry had sorted out the music into piles and closed the piano. It wasn't like him.

Cold fear clutched at his stomach and Joey hurried to the piano. With a crash, he pushed up the lid, expecting to find some note left on the keys. He wasn't sure what he expected. Something like, "I hate the piano"

216

or "Enough is enough" — the childish but direct kind of message he'd be inclined to print in large black letters himself. But there was no note.

Then he noticed that the wastebasket by the table was full — that same wicker wastebasket from which he'd pulled the old Christmas card and read his mother's letter. That had been almost like getting a printed fortune-telling card out of a weighing machine. Perhaps the wastebasket once again would provide a message.

He really expected nothing more than old letters from girls that Jerry had answered, or discarded notes for a paper he mentioned writing during vacation. But the first piece he looked at began, "Dear Mum: I couldn't seem to tell you or Dad during Christmas vacation that I didn't want to go back to the Conservatory. I am not cut out to be a concert pianist after all. I just haven't got the extreme talent that it takes. And I don't want to settle for anything less — like teaching music. Do you think you can understand how I feel after years of dreaming this dream?"

That paper was torn and Joey couldn't find the matching piece. But he found a large piece crumpled fiercely into a fist of paper. He smoothed it out and read, "Dear Mum, I hate to let you and Dad down but this is to tell you that I am not going back to the Conservatory. It's far better to quit now and not waste everyone's time and go on to doing something else. The biggest problem is I haven't any idea of what. You

217

will want to know *why* I am quitting and I can only tell you it is because I am not good enough at what I want to do. I always goof at the crucial moment. This is terrible because I still dream of really being my dream — the pianist I'd always hoped to be."

A paragraph was heavily scratched out and when Joey read on, his hand shook and he could hardly believe his eyes.

Jerry continued, "I should have written you that after vacation I got so depressed that I couldn't eat and I couldn't play, in addition to not being able to sleep. So I was sent to a psychiatrist, Dr. Blake, who is connected with the school. He saw me three times and then said he thought I ought to get in touch with you or Dad, but I just couldn't make myself do it. I couldn't make myself do anything. I still thought maybe it was the accident to my fingers that slowed me down. I'm sure I played better at home last summer. But Dr. Blake told me yesterday morning that my real problem is to stop trying to be a perfectionist. But he can't tell me how to stop. And that doesn't make sense, because any great pianist *must* be a perfectionist. So I am trapped. He told me to come home and talk to you. But I don't think I can explain this very well talking. Somehow I just can't talk to anyone. So I'm trying to write it instead. But when I read it over it doesn't make much sense either, and not just because it's six o'clock in the morning and I haven't been able to sleep here at home either."

Then Jerry had crunched the paper up. Other papers in the basket were notes for an essay on Baroque music, torn into emphatic strips, as if each rip had been a rending of his self.

Joey looked around the room again and on the floor by Jerry's bed he saw a glass with a few drops of water left in the bottom and a bottle of pills. He remembered Jerry's scoffing once when Joey had asked for something stronger than aspirin for a toothache. "Who needs pills? Just turn on some nice music and relax. Don't you know they even have Music To Be Operated On By now?"

But Jerry could no longer take his own advice. So what had he taken? Joey turned the bottle around and read the prescription. "Jeremy Larkin — take one or two for sleep if absolutely necessary Dr. Blake." The bottle still had nine or ten pills in it, but it must have had many more when it was full. Jerry had obviously taken some, but how many? and when? It must have been in the last couple of hours — after he couldn't sleep. After he tried writing those letters.

Joey decided he had to find Jerry and see if he was all right. He ran for his jacket and cap. Jock in his too-big pajamas stood blinking in the doorway of his room.

"I thought you were suppposed to wake me up and cook me my breakfast and see I got to school on time. You should have done it half an hour ago."

"You'll just have to do it yourself," Joey told him grimly. "You can still make your school before it begins."

"Are you going to your exam now?"

"No. I'm not. I have to do something else. Now grow up and take care of yourself today."

"Joey! Are you playing hookey? From your exams? Dad will never forgive you."

"I am not deliberately playing hookey. If I can get to school before the exam begins, I will." He banged the door shut behind him. Then he opened it again and yelled, "And don't *you* touch Bertie in the box. Leave him alone."

He shut the door quickly again before Jock, shocked at that news, could react.

For once he wished for a fresh fall of snow so there would be tracks to follow. But the driveway was plowed to the road; the shoveled paths were pock marked with prints. And where Reino walked toward the woods there were four or five days of old tracks. Reino had already passed that way because there was a distant buzz of a saw.

Was Jerry just clearing his head after a groggy night? Or what? And where had he gone?

Joey walked slowly down the front path to the drive-

220

way, letting the cold air and sharp sun slice at him. Then without hesitation he turned toward the woods. That was where he went for solace. Or for a hike. Jerry probably would still do the same.

He stepped briskly. The snow was old and deceptively crusty. Just when he thought it was hard, he would sink through into snow that was still a foot deep. But in a few minutes he passed the pond and the woods seemed to reach out and embrace him. It was a funny feeling — as if the woods were alive and waiting for him, and he was the uncommitted one, waiting to see what would happen, where some kind of fate or instinct would prod him.

He followed the footsteps where Reino's large boots had broken out the path. Brown oak leaves caught in some of the holes. But there seemed to be no side tracks.

Then Joey's breath caught and a claw of pain scraped in his stomach. Stuck in one of the footprints was a slipper sock. He picked it up and found the leather sole stiff with cold and the knit top wet from the chilling snow. He knew it was Jerry's. He knew Jerry had come this way — maybe only ten minutes before. And now he realized something was really horribly wrong. Jerry must be dazed, because in his right mind he would never take to the woods in slipper socks. What else would he have on? Pajamas? A coat?

"Help me find Jerry!" Joey whispered, almost unaware it was a prayer — unaddressed, but a message of terror and anxiety. "Help me find Jerry."

Watching the snow on each side of the path, Joey hurried on. But he knew where he would look first: the X on the map, the secret place of dreams and long thoughts and hopes that hadn't died, the big rock in the green tower of cedars.

Savagely he pushed through the prickly barrier of branches and, suddenly seeing Jerry, took a great gulping breath. His brother sat on the crystal ice crust atop the rock, arms around his thin knees, his long-fingered hands raw with cold and his head bowed on his knees. One foot was bare, but his partly open trench coat covered an old pair of pajamas. His face, turned toward Joey, was slack and his eyes were closed.

"Jerry!" Joey shouted. He dug his fingernails into the slippery ice-coated stone and pulled his way up. He grabbed Jerry's shoulder and shook until his brother's neck seemed to snap. Jerry's eyes opened, dull and lost.

"Couldn't sleep," muttered Jerry. "Couldn't sleep."

"But you took some pills. How many, Jerry? How many?"

"Two to oncet once," said Jerry, irrationally quoting an old family remark which had become a counting joke. "And then two to oncet again, maybe, or three because I forgot the first or they didn't work. But I couldn't sleep. And now I can't wake up."

"Oh, yes you can!" Joey got a grip under Jerry's arms and hauled him to his feet. But his brother's heavy eyelids fell shut. Joey saw him — empty-faced and empty-eyed as if he didn't know who was inside. It was like the little rabbit locked inside himself before his eyes opened.

"The air will wake you up. Let's get off the rock and you can keep awake walking. Help me, Jerry. Wake up and slide off the rock."

But his brother sagged against him and couldn't seem to make himself move. Joey tried yelling, "Reino!" hoping the man would hear, but the saw screamed on.

"Well, a few bruises won't hurt." Joey let Jerry's limp body down until he was stretched out on the rock. He pulled the slipper sock he'd plucked from the path onto Jerry's bare foot, and then bracing himself he held Jerry's arms and slid him over the edge of the rock into the trees. While Joey scrambled off, Jerry kept on sliding down, crumbling through the green branches until he collapsed on the snow. Joey pulled and hauled until he got him out to the path. Even though Jerry was slight, his dead weight was awkward. Joey panted and his breath was knife-sharp in his chest.

"Jerry! Take a step. We're going home. Answer me, Jerry. Take a step." He pulled his brother's arm over his shoulder and held him up as best he could.

"Can't sleep," said Jerry. "Want to sleep for a week. For a year. That's all I want."

"No you don't!" snapped Joey. "The minute you realized you'd taken more pills than you meant to you headed right outdoors! You don't want to sleep, Jerry, and you know it — or you wouldn't have come out to clear your head. It was an accident you took too many. Now fight it."

"That's right. Didn't mean to," Jerry agreed. He took a few steps until inertia overcame him again and his head fell forward. His weight poured over Joey like the settling of a sandbag.

Joey stood still in the path. He waited until the saw screeched sharply and then stopped. He called "Reino!" three times so loudly he thought his larynx would burst. But he heard no reply. Then the saw began again.

So Joey had to decide by himself what was best. Would the freezing air clear Jerry's head before pneumonia or frostbite could claim a hold? Or was it a matter of rushing him home and calling a doctor to take over?

Joey decided if the cold air were going to help it would have by now. Even standing in the snow didn't make him want to lift his feet. Perhaps the cold just numbed them. He'd better try home and Dr. Harvey before it was too late.

He scooched down and hauled Jerry over his shoulder in a fireman's carry. Now, with the added weight, he sank into the foot of snow with every step. And every step became a greater strain. He began saying to himself, "One foot up and over and ahead of the other. One foot up and over — "

When he came out of the woods, he had to stop a moment and prop Jerry against a tree. Jerry groaned, but he didn't try to talk. As Joey heaved him once more over his shoulder, he heard the front door bang and saw Jock stamping down the driveway to the road. Jock was in a temper because no one had taken care of him that morning. He didn't look back to see that Joey needed help. And for all Joey was tempted to call out, to stop him and yell for him to go phone Dr. Harvey, he decided maybe Jock was too young for this. Besides he didn't even know Jerry had come home late last night. He wouldn't understand anything and it would upset him. Then he would whine and be a baby and cause trouble and ask for needless attention from everyone. No, it was easier for Joey to handle this alone.

By the time he reached the driveway his feet were heavy as millstones and his knees were shot with pain at each step. His breath came in searing gasps between the hammer blows of his heartbeats. If only Jock hadn't decided to be smart and lock the front door!

Joey grasped the handle and found that he had. Gently he set Jerry down on the step and raced for the outside door by the Music Room. That too had a snap lock that had shut tight when Jerry left.

He knew he hadn't unlocked the kitchen that morning or touched the door to the screened porch for days. It meant smashing a window over the terrace. From the garage he grabbed up a tire iron and running back to the glassed-in passage took a swing at a window. The glass sprang through the air, sparkling in the sun like tingling fireworks.

Joey smashed out three jagged pieces so he could crawl through. He couldn't remember Dr. Harvey's phone number and there wasn't any book by the kitchen phone, so he called the operator.

"Please get hold of Dr. Paul Harvey at once and ask him to hurry to the Larkin place at the end of Adams Road. It's an emergency."

"Do you need the police or an ambulance?" the operator asked.

"Not now. Just Dr. Harvey. But quick." He hung up and raced through the hall, opening the front door. Jerry was slumped just as Joey left him. He hauled him into the house, leaving the front door wide open, and pulled him out to the kitchen, where he propped him in a chair. He put water on to boil and dumped four huge teaspoonfuls of instant coffee into a mug.

In three minutes he was trying to force spoonfuls of coffee into Jerry and then was frantic as Jerry made no effort to swallow it. Panic crept in insidious little ways along Joey's nerves and into his mind. He wanted to screech at Jerry and hit him. He wanted to scream, "Help!" so loudly that in faraway New York his parents would hear, and in whatever corner of heaven or soul there was a power to help, his despair would be answered.

Exhausted, he sat down and put his head in his hands. He barely heard the footsteps as Dr. Harvey came into the house on the run, calling, "Who's here?"

"In the kitchen," Joey croaked and pointed to Jerry. "He took sleeping pills, and he was real mixed up about how many — and then he went outdoors, and I can't wake him up."

Dr. Harvey was busy, checking and feeling and prodding. "Where's your mother?"

"In New York. Reino's in the woods. Jock's in school."

"Well, we've got him in time. But he needs some work. Come with me in the car and we'll get him up to the hospital. Grab some blankets. You sit in the back seat and hold him up and talk to him. I think somehow he'll hear you. Just keep talking."

So Joey held Jerry as the car swerved through the ice and shook them from side to side, and he talked. "Remember the time you pitched the no-hitter for the Little League, Jerry? And when it was all over and Dad said you could have anything you wanted — "

How had he started on that one? That was when Jerry said all he wanted was to quit Little League now he'd proved himself and to have all the time he needed for his own pursuits. And he'd meant the piano.

But somehow Joey rattled on and they reached the emergency entrance. And this time it was Joey, not his mother, who answered the questions in the Admitting Office, while Dr. Harvey and the nurses rushed Jerry into a small room out of sight.

"Now, was this an accident?" asked the clerk.

"Oh, yes. It was very definitely an accident. I think I'd better call my parents and tell them."

"There's a pay phone in the corridor," said the girl.

Joey went to the phone before he realized he had no money. His wallet with his bus pass and change lay on the hall table with his pen and extra ink cartridges for the exam. Above him he saw a clock and he couldn't believe that the hands said only eight-forty-five. In fifteen minutes his French exam began. But he couldn't get there in time, even if he ran all the way from the hospital to the high school. And he was so drained of energy he couldn't think of one word in French. It was hopeless.

After half an hour, Dr. Harvey came out of the room and looked around.

"You want me?" Joey called.

"I just want to tell you Jerry will be all right. We've pumped his stomach, and he's getting the right stimulants and so forth. Joe, come along and tell me what's been going on here. I've seldom seen an intelligent, usually well-nourished young man, who should be in good physical condition, in such a weak and un-

228

dernourished state. Do you know anything about what Jerry's been up to?"

He led Joey down the hall and into the doctor's lounge. With relief, Joey poured out all he knew, from Jerry's troubled talk at Christmas to the letter about the psychiatrist's advice, and the final events from midnight to now.

"You say your parents didn't have an inkling about all this? And now they're at the Plaza in New York? I think I'll phone your father and have a talk with him. Or do you want to talk to him or your mother?"

Joey shook his head. "No. I'm supposed to be taking a French mid-year right now. And I've got a math exam at two o'clock. And I just can't take them! I haven't got my bus pass or any money or pens or anything with me. I left them all at home." His voice broke and Joey was surprised and embarrassed at his sudden outburst.

Dr. Harvey gave Joey's appearance serious consideration. "Perhaps you shouldn't try to take exams today."

"I can't seem to think at all. I'm really shook up — not just over what happened to Jerry, but why it happened. I don't understand it. Maybe it would have been better if I'd never found his fingertip last summer. Maybe I just made things tougher for him."

"You've got one of the most well-developed senses of responsibility I've seen in a boy your age, Joe. But you mustn't let it run away with you. You found Jerry's fingertip and I sewed it back on. But what he does with it — or doesn't do with it — is not *our* responsibility. Each person is responsible for what he does all by himself. You must never blame anyone else for what you do or you don't do. And as for what happens to you, you have to learn to accept some things and then do the best you can."

Joey thought and agreed. "You mean Jerry's responsible for his own actions no matter what I did. And the only person responsible for my actions is me."

"Right." said Dr. Harvey with a smile. "But you can take the credit for saving your brother's life. If you hadn't found him as quickly as you did, he probably would have caught pneumonia or even have died of exposure. He's lucky to have you for a brother."

"I hope he thinks so. He has a terrible problem to work out. I guess it's because he's lost his faith in himself. I'm really better off, because I never had much faith in myself anyway!" Joey grinned and tried to sound flip.

"But you can't say that any more. You've got more faith in yourself than you realize. You see, you've proved yourself twice in emergencies. You know, people talk about heroes and say that the days of great heroes have passed. We used to have knights and explorers and men who could do great things that kind of shook the world into shape. But we still have heroes today — and it's harder because they fight unknowns."

"What do you mean, unknowns?"

"They have to fight things like fear of the bomb and fear of losing faith with life and what it's all about. Why, life is the greatest gift we get in this world! So we have to fight the things that happen to our minds and our spirits as well as our bodies. If we don't use our life, if we just sit around all afraid and whine about the state of our minds and the state of the world, we've lost the meaning of life. It's up to us — each one of us — to make the most of his own life."

It was a lot of thought to absorb and Joey still looked a little harassed by too much happening all at once.

"Look here, before I phone your parents let me try to catch that young doctor who boards at a house down at the foot of Adams Road. He's just going off duty and he'll be glad to give you a lift. I'd recommend that you go home and relax for a few hours. If anybody complains that you missed exams, tell them to call me."

The young doctor insisted on dropping Joey off at his front door. "You're sure you're all right? Want me to come in with you?"

"No, thanks. I'm all right. I may even go take my math exam. It would be awful to have two exams to make up. I'll see how I feel."

"Okay, kid!" The doctor tried to turn a yawn into a grin and rushed off.

To his dismay, Joey had to climb through the window again, as he'd slammed the door shut on their hurried departure and his key was still inside. He supposed he ought to fetch Reino to board up the window before the cold air gushing in ruined his mother's plants.

But first he needed hot cocoa. His whole inside felt scraped and empty, as if he were completely hollow from his toes to his scalp.

Wearily he entered the kitchen. The first thing he saw was a note crayoned in huge hateful red letters by Jock and pinned to the bulletin board. It read: *Mum —I am late to school because Joel ignored me this morning, was abrupt and spiteful and furthermore he has not gone to his exams. I think it's because Bertie came back all sick. You shouldn't let him keep that animal again. Love, Jock.*

Joey saw the box on the kitchen table, just as he left it. But he dreaded looking inside to see what shape his friend was in. Why did everything awful happen at once?

9

JOEY HEATED some milk, leaving a little in the pan to spoon into Bertie. Then he mixed his cocoa and drank without really tasting it.

He stared at the box, remembering the other time Bertie had been hurt. But that had been Bertie's doing, that leap into space after a teasing bird.

He remembered the next time Bertie was hurt and how he had hugged the raccoon so tightly, feeling the furry warmth against his own shivering body. But that had been his father's doing, that wicked swing with the hockey stick.

Now he stared at the box and thought that whatever terrible things had happened to Bertie in these four weeks had been his fault. Or had it! Dr. Harvey had made it pretty emphatic about responsibility. He wondered if Bertie, given the gift of thought, would have blamed Joey for his circumstances or, at the time of his release, rejoiced in his freedom and made the best of it. He would never know. But now he had to accept what lay before him.

He made himself bend over the box. Gently he stroked a finger over the outline of the raccoon's black mask. There was a tiny twitch to Bertie's ears and a flick of his eyes, half-opening for a second. Carefully Joey managed to fit two or three spoonfuls of milk into his mouth.

But afterwards Joey did stand there, wondering, "Am I doing the right thing? Am I helping in a tough spot — or making it worse?"

His eyes caught Jock's note again and in sudden frustration, badgered by all the things that seemed unjust — missing his exam, Jock's complaints, the dilemma both emotional and physical of Bertie — he suddenly grabbed his cocoa mug and flung it with all his strength against the floor. The mug, decorated with blue Peter Rabbits, had been a relic of his childhood, but how unfamiliar it looked in pieces. How unfamiliar everything was at that moment. He even felt as if he stood there with jagged pieces of himself in his hands. Being the only one responsible for his own actions was the toughest responsibility of all!

He picked up the shards of the mug. He supposed he could glue it together so it would look all right, but it would never be useful again. Quickly he dumped the pieces in the trash. He was rather ashamed. He realized it hadn't really been so different from his father's furious swing at Bertie with a hockey stick. It hadn't solved anything.

For a long time he just stood there trying to think things out, but he couldn't seem to find any answers. Then he realized he wasn't really doing much but stare at the kitchen clock. When the facts on its face finally reached him he was surprised at how fast the morning was running away from him. He should find Reino.

This time it was hard walking in the woods. The urgency of his earlier search was gone and he felt tired. He was even out of breath by the time he reached the stand of pines where Reino worked, and he couldn't talk.

"Did you get up late and miss your exam?" Reino glared at him. "Should I have stayed around and pounded you awake and cooked your breakfast for you, you lazy lunk!"

Joey shook his head. "I wish that's all it was," he finally gasped.

Reino put down his small branch-trimming saw. "Sit

down. Get your breath. I'll pour you some coffee." Reino reached for his thermos.

Joey didn't want the coffee. Reino always made it bitter as witches' brew and drank it straight. But it was Reino's cure-all, just as his mother's was a good cup of tea. So he accepted it.

Neither did Joey know how to begin — in which order to pour out his troubles. Now that Jerry was safe, Bertie seemed the worst problem.

"Well," said Reino, "something must be wrong. You look like you'd lost your best friend."

"That's about it. Bertie came back last night. He was almost dead when I found him on the doorstep. He is alive this morning, but this time he's in real tough shape. I probably shouldn't let him suffer any longer."

"I never thought he'd come back!" Reino spoke in amazement. "Not after all that time. And he's hurt bad?"

"He might have been hit by a car and dragged himself here. Or chewed up by dogs."

"He might have had a fight with other raccoons," Reino told him. "After the life he'd led, he could have been an outcast among his own kind."

"Don't rub it in. I know I never should have kept him." For a moment the thoughts he'd heard and worked on that morning fled from his mind. "I ruined his whole life!"

"Did Bertie tell you that?"

"How could Bertie tell me anything!"

"He told you a lot — by coming back to you. He told you that he needed you and he trusted you and he loved you. Think of it that way."

"That makes it worse," Joey choked. "Because I don't know what to do with him now."

"Let's go back and see." Reino started to leave his lunch box and his tools.

"Maybe we'd better bring your stuff back to the house. You might not get back here today. There's a window to board up. And if I go up to that exam, I think someone ought to stick around the house."

"Look here, Joe. Did you miss that early exam just on account of Bertie — or is there something else?"

"There's Jerry."

As they walked, Joey told Reino the complete history of last night and this morning. Reino pushed his cap back off his forehead, as he always did when he was perplexed. Joey used to wonder if he did it to let in a supply of fresh air so he could think better.

"I never would have believed Jerry could give up that piano. I thought his music was built right into him. He must have been having a terrible time. What's he going to do now?"

"Face up to Dad, I guess."

"Poor fellow. No, I won't say that. Because he's got a reason for what he's doing. It's going to be harder on your Dad, who won't understand that reason very well, if you don't mind my saying so."

"I don't mind," Joey agreed. "Dr. Harvey gave me a speech this morning on accepting things. Maybe he ought to give the same speech to Dad. But Dad sure fits the other part of his speech!"

"What's that?"

"Making the most out of life. Dad doesn't want to miss anything. Or have us miss anything."

"What your Dad's got to learn is to let you boys live your life your own way. He can't live it for you — or give it to you all packaged up neat!"

"I think he's tried to tell us that all along," Joey discovered. "That each of us has to live his own life and do his own deeds. Oh, boy! That's right back to what Dr. Harvey said this morning, only it just never got through to me before. And now I can see something else, too."

"What's that?"

"Dad just has so much going for him that he can't help trying to help us too much. He could tell me, 'It's up to you,' but when I couldn't come through the way he thought I should, he'd worry and get anxious and try to pull strings to help. Like that school in Scotland bit. Oh, boy!" said Joey again. "Have I been thick. I just couldn't admit that everything is really up to me."

"That's right," said Reino. "You just get out there

and do what you can and there's good times and there's bad. So you stick with it, but you thank God for the good times." As they came to the house, Reino saw the broken window. "When you decide to clobber something, you really do it, Joe."

"I'd stick around and help you fix it. But I've got to take that math exam."

"You better had!" Reino cheered him on.

One good thing about the math exam was that it absorbed his mind completely for two whole hours. But as he left the room he had the bad luck to bump into his French teacher.

"Why, Joel Larkin — I thought you must be ill. You didn't take my French II exam this morning."

"I know. I wasn't sick, but I just couldn't be there."

"Did your mother or father notify the school?"

"No. They aren't home."

"You overslept? Or you just didn't feel like bothering to take a French exam?"

"I couldn't come. But I'll take the make-up exam whenever you say."

"If you weren't ill and cannot hand in a signed excuse from a parent who was there and knew why you did not appear, I see no reason to allow you a make-up exam. You will just receive F for the half-year. We don't encourage students to miss exams out of sheer whimsey."

"It wasn't whimsey," said Joey. "Please, I've got to

239

take that exam and pass it. So I don't have to go away to school."

She looked as if nothing would please her more than to have Joel Larkin, the frozen-tongued, accentless, verbless bane of her classes transferred to another school. But she also saw a purposeful look in Joey's eyes, replacing the uneasy diffidence she'd always felt from him before.

"Very well. Talk to the Principal on Monday. If he agrees you have a legitimate excuse, you may have a make-up."

When he went home, to his great surprise he found Jock in the kitchen doing dishes which had accumulated during the day's odd snacks. The red crayoned note was no longer on the bulletin board.

"I'm sorry I was cross at you," Jock said. "Reino told me what happened. But why didn't you tell me what was going on then? I could have helped you look. I could have figured out statistically the chances of where Jerry would be most apt to go."

"I'm sure you could. But instinct is quicker than statistics. And I didn't think you'd ever bothered to look up *X-sh!* on the map."

"Oh, I hadn't. It didn't seem to be a fact I'd need at any time. Anyway, I took the note down. Mum called from the airport in Boston. They're going to see Jerry at the hospital and then they'll be home."

"What did you do with Bertie's box?"

"Reino put it out of the way in your room."

"Oh? You mean — "

"Bertie's still alive, Reino says. But he didn't want any milk. He's just sort of breathing, that's all. I had to keep walking by him in here and it bothered me. So I told Reino, and he moved him. I don't like to see anything like that."

"Who does?" Joey asked. But he stopped short of needling Jock. Last week he probably would have asked, "What's the matter with your great scientific curiosity?"

But before he could go and look at the raccoon, they heard the slam of car doors. Jock rushed to the front door and threw it open, and then backed up and stepped on Joey.

"Jerry's with them! What should I say to him!"

"Just say 'Hi,' for heaven's sakes, and don't make a big thing out of it."

In their attempt to make it all as normal as possible, the boys were so restrained that it hardly seemed a fitting homecoming for Mr. Larkin. And he was so preoccupied with his thoughts that he gave a routine greeting to the boys.

Mrs. Larkin rumpled Jock's spikey hair, but it was Joey she hugged. She didn't say anything, yet he had the feeling she was clinging to him.

"How was the trip, Mum?"

"Oh, Joel! That's a practical question!" She

241

laughed, but it sounded tinny. "It was fun until Dr. Harvey finally reached us at the hotel this morning. Then, even with the short plane trip, I thought we'd never get here. I'm glad Dad could come with me. He just told the company he could not go off to South America until things were straightened out at home."

Jerry, still in his pajamas, raincoat and slipper socks, gave Joey a faint grin and said quietly, "Mind if I sneak into your room and read in there for a while?"

"No. Go ahead."

"Come in when you get a chance."

Joey nodded. "Jock tells me Reino put Bertie in there. He's in a box, but he's pretty well chewed up. I'm coming to check on him as soon as I can."

In the confusion of getting the luggage out of the way and coats hung up, Jerry's calm exit wasn't noticed until Mum suddenly asked, "Jerry! Where'd he go?"

"He's gone to read in my room. You know, I could sleep down in the Music Room for a while. Why don't I just tell Jerry to stay there for now?"

"That would be good of you, Joel. I'd like to be near Jerry. If he needs me."

"How come Dr. Harvey let him come home?" Jock asked. "I thought Jerry was sick."

"He might catch a bad cold," explained Mrs. Larkin. "But that's no reason to keep him in the hospital when he didn't want to stay there. Dr. Harvey says he can rest just as well at home and eat more often."

Mr. Larkin turned his attention to Joey. "What I don't understand is that you knew — since Christmas vacation — that Jerry was upset. Why didn't you tell us?"

"Because he asked me not to."

"Jock, we're going in the library and have a conversation. Why don't you go do your homework and I'll come and tell you about my trip later?" Mr. Larkin dispatched Jock without giving him time for a quivered lip. Then he ushered Joey into the library and Mrs. Larkin followed.

"But if you knew your brother needed help, wouldn't it have made sense to tell us anyway?"

"I didn't know he needed help that badly, or that he'd been sent to a psychiatrist. All I knew was that he felt he was in the wrong place and he didn't have courage enough to tell you, Dad, that he wanted out."

Mr. Larkin was perplexed. "All I've ever done is encourage you kids. I'm all for you! Whatever you want to do. But instead of my encouraging you, it looks as if I'd intimidated you."

He sat down heavily on the arm of a chair and stared at Joey.

Joey stared back at him and for the first time he found he wasn't in awe of him or afraid of what his father would say. He was looking at a sorely puzzled man. The love which Joey doubted he could ever feel for his father again suddenly surged back.

"Oh, I don't think that, Dad. You just want things for us so badly. But they won't happen unless we get around to wanting them, too, and working for them by ourselves."

Mr. Larkin couldn't seem to think of anything else to say or, if he did, the best way to say it. Joey didn't want to tell him anything else. He had a feeling his father was going to learn a lot the hard way, talking to Jerry.

"Do you want me any more?"

"Not right this minute," said Mr. Larkiin.

"Joel," said his mother, "we both want to thank you for finding Jerry when you did. If you hadn't—" Her voice shrank away.

"Oh, Mum! It turned out all right, didn't it?"

She turned her back, but Joey knew it was because she didn't want to embarrass him by crying.

"I'll be around if you want me," Joey said and left his parents to talk things out for themselves.

Jerry was sitting up in Joey's bed, a book against his knees.

"How do you feel?" Joey asked.

"Okay. I never want to have my stomach pumped out again, though. That's awful! Dr. Harvey told me to rest today but tomorrow I can do anything I want. Even play the piano."

"Do that! After all this! Are you some kind of nut?"

"Probably," Jerry laughed. "I may want to go back

to the Conservatory in a year, after I know a little more about myself. I had a long talk with Dr. Harvey before Mum and Dad came."

"Did he give you a speech on responsibility and accepting things?"

"No. He talked about making the most out of life, but keeping things in proportion. You know, the laughs are as important as the groans and so forth."

"I guess he's got different speeches for different people."

"That's what he said. Everybody sees his own problem differently, and you give each person a different prescription."

"I wish I knew what prescription to give Bertie." Joey saw that Reino had left the box by the window.

He went over to look. At first he couldn't tell if Bertie were dead or alive. He felt as breathless and motionless as the raccoon's body. Then he picked up Bertie's scarred paw. When he let it go, it fell back against the soft fur without a sigh of sound.

There was nothing left of Joey's joy but a battered body in a box.

"Is he dead?" Jerry asked.

"He's dead. And I wish I'd never seen him like this!" Joey said savagely.

"I'm sorry, Joe. What a rotten day this is. No — what a rotten year, I guess. Too bad we can't go back and do it all over again some other way."

"Rotten and mixed-up is right," Joey agreed. He stared out the window.

But suddenly in his mind he saw Bertie running through the woods, chasing autumn leaves and catching snowflakes and jumping into puddles — full of the joy of life.

"No. I wouldn't want to do it all over again any other way," he decided. "Except for the ending. I'll always wish there was another ending for Bertie."

He picked up the box and took it away.